Chef

CEE BOWERMAN

BOOK THREE

Professionally edited by Chrissy Riesenberg

CEE BOWERMAN BOOK LIST

Texas Knights MC

Home Forever

Forever Family

Lucky Forever

Love Forever

Texas Kings MC

Kale

Sonny

Bird

Grunt

Lout

Smokey

Tucker

Kale & Terra (Novella)

John & Mattie

Bear

Daughtry

Hank

Fain

Grady

Stoffer

Luke - COMING AUGUST 2021!

Conner Brothers Construction

Finn

Angus

Mace

Ronan

Royal

Rojo, TX

Rason & Eliza

Atlas & Addie

Jazmyne & Luc

Time Served MC

Boss

Hook

Chef

Tempests

Wrath

Please follow Cee on Facebook, Instagram, and Twitter.

Also, for information on new releases and to catch up with Cee, go to www.ceebowermanbooks.com

A NOTE FROM THE AUTHOR

Dear Reader,

I'm excited to bring you Chef and Brea's story! Brea's was inspired by my friend Pickle. (The rest of the world calls her Brea, but she's my Pickle.) Imagine that, right? First, I introduced you to my friend Jenn, then Paula, and now you can get to know Brea and her daughter, Sis.

I have been lucky enough to get to know Brea over the last year and am happy to call her my friend. The funniest part of that is that I've never actually met her in person, just talked to her for hours by messenger and on video chat with our crazy coven of women - that also includes Jenn, Paula, and Ciara.

Occasionally, I get to chat with Sis, Brea's daughter, who never fails to make me smile. I was happy to add her to my Time Served crew of strong and funny ladies and love that I can give her all the wild and crazy pets she wants. Now, I've just got to find a way to get that girl an otter . . . I checked into a live one, but that's not in my budget just yet, and I'm pretty sure Brea would hire a hitman if I found a way to make it happen.

It might be worth it, though, just to see Sis smile.

Someday soon, I'll get to meet Brea and Sis because ages ago I promised to teach Sis how to ride a motorcycle. As soon as we can sync our schedules, I'll make sure that happens. For now, I'll be content with my chats with the girls and occasional glimpses of Sis when she pops onto the screen.

I'm glad that I've been able to bring my friends to life in the pages of my books and give them each a wild history and steamy love story with the man of their dreams.

I saw a meme on FB the other day that said it best - *A good friend knows all your stories. A best friend helped you create them.* That's what my girls have done for me, and I have faith that they'll keep doing it and pushing me to create more of the books my readers seem to enjoy.

Happy reading,

Cee

PROLOGUE

FIVE YEARS AGO

CHEF

"What are you doing out here?" I heard a woman's voice ask from somewhere in the dark to my right. I waited for a second, not sure if she was talking to me since I'd thought I was hidden out here, away from the party going on in front of Pop's. "Hello? Can you hear me, or am I talking to myself?"

"Are you always that sarcastic when you talk to yourself?" I asked the voice.

"You should hear the voices in my head. When they get going, sarcasm is the least of my problems."

"The voices in your head talk to you?"

"Don't yours?"

"I don't have voices, sweetheart. You might want to get that checked out."

"You don't have an inner dialogue? Right now, there's not some voice in your head saying, 'I don't know who this girl is, but she's fucking nuts!' or something?"

I did, actually, but I wasn't sure I wanted to admit it to a still-faceless woman who was hiding out in the dark talking to me. Hell, maybe I did have voices in my head, but mine were manifesting as some woman in a junkyard talking to me in the moonlight.

"Come out where I can see you," I ordered.

"Technically, I came out here to be alone but then I came across you. You scared me to death!" the girl said as she walked closer. With only the light of the moon, I could barely make out her features, but I could see enough to see she was young. Very young. The compound I lived in was not the place that some young, innocent kid belonged.

I'd only been out of prison for a week, and in that time, I'd slowly started to get settled in my new place - a modest one-bedroom house next to a junkyard surrounded by other small houses that were occupied by convicts just like me. Some of the men had been out for a bit while others hadn't been free much longer than I had.

All of us had been convicted and sentenced by a court of law and served time in the Texas prison system. I didn't know their back stories and didn't care to. I just wanted to have a place to call home until I could figure out what the fuck I was going to do with my life outside the prison walls I'd been behind for the last five years.

"You ought to be scared, little girl. Does your mama know where you are and who you're associating with?"

The girl laughed softly and nudged me over so she could sit down next to me on a ratty seat someone had pulled out of one of the junk cars.

"First, at 22, I'm not a little girl. Second, she knows I'm somewhere on the property and doesn't have a problem with it. I work out here now, but I've been hanging out with big old baddies like you since I was a teenager. My parents are here for the cookout. I think my mom is schooling Boss, Hook, and a few of the new guys in cards right now. My dad isn't playing because he's smart enough to know better than to bet against her. The other guys haven't learned their lesson yet."

"Your dad used to live here?"

"Nope. Dad's never even had a parking ticket, let alone served time. Have you started building your bike yet?"

"How'd you know that?" I asked. Just this morning, Pop had shown up at my door with a mug full of coffee and told me not to make plans for tomorrow afternoon because we were going to be building my motorcycle. How he thought a man my size - a black man, no less - belonged on the back of a motorcycle was beyond me. That was some crazy shit white men did, ride around with the wind blowing in their hair saying 'fuck you' to the man or something stupid like that.

I didn't want to say 'fuck you' to *the man*. I didn't want to talk to him or anyone else. However, this little tiny thing wouldn't shut up and leave me the hell alone.

"Did you just growl at me?" the girl asked before she started laughing. I didn't know if she was laughing at me or if she thought she was laughing with me. Either way, I wanted her gone.

"Why don't you run along, little girl? I'm not the kind of man you want as a friend."

"Probably not. You seem awfully prickly." I wasn't looking at her, but I felt her shrug. She didn't take the hint and just kept right on talking. "Back to the motorcycle. Did you and Pop talk about what style you want? It's got to be a Harley. There's just no sense in it being anything else. As big as you are . . ."

I listened to the girl drone on about engine sizes, motorcycle styles, something about the angle of a rake, and I finally had to interrupt her. "How do you know all this shit anyway, kid? Better yet, *why* do you know all this shit? Are you recruiting for that motorcycle gang they've got going?"

"It's not a gang. People like you have to avoid any type of gang affiliations, right?" The girl nudged me with her elbow again before laughing at her own joke. "I know about this stuff because that's what I do. I know things. And I want a motorcycle of my own someday."

"What the hell for?"

"You've never ridden on a motorcycle, have you?"

"Nope."

"You'll understand once you do."

"Doubtful."

"I'll make a deal with you. When you love it and prove me right, you'll help me convince Hook and Boss to let me build a bike of my own."

"What do I win if you're wrong?"

"I won't be, so it doesn't matter."

"You do see that the whole scenario is unbalanced, right? If I hate it, I hate it. If I somehow love it, you get a motorcycle out of the deal."

"Well, then, what do you want?"

"Some peace and fucking quiet?"

"You're a really cranky guy, mister. How about I not shut up until you walk back over to the fire with me, and let me whoop *you* at cards. My mom taught me how to play."

"You're not going to leave me alone, are you?"

"Nope," the girl assured me with a sigh. "I just don't have it in me to drop things. Mom says I'm like a dog with a bone and don't know how to stop when I'm ahead."

"From where I'm sitting, your mom sounds like the smartest one in your family. Does she have voices in her head too? I understand shit like that can be genetic."

"Are you bald because you shave your head or because of your old age? Did you know that the mother's genes are what determines the children's hair? At least the thickness and stuff. Also, if a woman has thin hair, it's likely her daughters will, too, and her sons will end up prematurely bald."

"What?" I stared at the girl beside me, shocked at the abrupt turn in the conversation.

"Should I talk slower, or am I sitting on the side without the hearing aid?"

"I . . . I . . . who the fuck are you?"

"I'm Sis, Brea's daughter. What's your name?"

"Marques Green."

"*The* Marques Green?"

"As far as I know, there's only one of me, or do you have some useless data about that shit too?"

"Marques Green that played for TSU and was drafted into the NFL his junior year where he still holds the record for most sacks in a season?" Shit. The kid knew football. At least that was a subject I knew something about. If she insisted on talking to me, we'd have to steer it that way. I could talk football and science because for most of my life, that was all I lived and breathed. Maybe if I started snapping data at her, she'd leave me the fuck alone so I could sit here in peace. I needed to figure out where the fuck my life was going and if it was even worth living at all. "Are you really *that* Marques Green?"

"One and the same, but you forgot that I've added to my resume. I got injured, took an early retirement, and went to prison for five years."

"Whatever," the girl scoffed as she waved her hand as if to brush away my prison record. "Now, that game against Cleveland where you picked the QB up and carried him for 10 yards, *that's* what you need to list on your resume. My dad . . ."

I scooted my ass closer to the edge of the seat and leaned my head back so I could stare up at the stars. Apparently, I'd made a new friend whether I wanted one or not, but at least now I had someone to talk football with.

CEE BOWERMAN

"Dad! You're never gonna believe who this is! Just guess!"

Sis, the little chatterbox who'd tagged me as her new toy, yelled as she dragged me over to the fire and card table where there were a group of people playing. There was a man sitting in a camp chair next to Pop who perked up when he saw the two of us walking toward him. He didn't seem at all shocked that his lily white girl was dragging a black man around by the hand. If anything, he seemed more than a little amused.

"Got you a live one there, Sis." Pop laughed as he watched us get closer to him. He shook his head and smiled at me. "She's hit or miss. Apparently, there's something about you that she connects with. Otherwise, she'd have hurt your feelings, and left you to cry about it."

"She adopted you, huh?" The other man interrupted the girl's chatter about my football career. "Well, welcome to the family. I'm her dad, Ray. Pull up a chair if you can get loose. Sis, let the man be, and run into the house and refill my glass, will you?"

The girl let my hand go and took the cup her father held out to her before she reached out for Pop's glass and asked, "You need me to top yours off, Pop?"

"Thanks, Sis." Pop held his glass out for her. The three of us were quiet as she walked away and then Pop nodded toward an empty chair and told me, "Take a load off, son. Join the family while we enjoy this pretty night under the stars."

13

I didn't feel like I had much choice, so I sat down in the chair even though I was worried it might not hold my weight.

"Sis ask you what you went in for?"

"No," I scoffed. "She doesn't seem to care. Not sure that's safe in this day and age, her walking up and starting a conversation with some stranger like me."

"You've got the highest body count out here currently, but you're not the meanest snake in the pit, by far," Pop said, completely unruffled by the fact that he was surrounded by ex-convicts. He turned to the man beside him and just blurted out my life story or the high points, at least. "This one here was a football star who became a science teacher at some high school down in Houston. Poor man lost his wife and then his daughter took the wrong path. When she died, he went to the school, cooked up a batch of poison, and unleashed it in some drug dealer's house. Stood right out there on the curb and watched them all crawl out coughing up their own blood. The fool was still standing there when the cops showed up."

I stared at Pop, angry that he was telling my story to some complete stranger who was probably going to judge me like everyone else.

"You poisoned their food? How did you get them to eat it?"

Because I was so pissed and wanted to get a reaction out of the guy, I told him, "That man was part of the reason I lost my daughter. Feeding him was not high on my list of priorities. I made a chemical solution and sealed it in an airtight canister with a valve release before I broke a window and tossed it into his fucking living room where he was sitting with a house full of other drug-dealing pimps and lowlifes."

"His body count was 14, but get this shit - he was found not guilty. Prosecutor was so fucking mad he'd lost the goddamn case that he brought him up on charges for misuse of state funds because he used the public school where he worked to cook his shit up."

"That's just reaching, right there," I heard a woman say as she walked past me and sat down in the man's lap next to Pop. "Are we ready to go home, honey? I took all their money again, and the guys are pissy. Where's Sis?"

"She went to refill our drinks but probably got sidetracked."

"I saw her walking toward the shop with Soda," the woman explained. She leaned forward and stuck her hand out and flashed the most breathtaking smile I'd ever seen and said, "Hi, I'm Brea. You must be this chef that the boys were talking about."

I reached out and took her hand. "That's me. I'm a chef."

I felt a jolt of electricity all the way up my arm when I touched her and had to shake my head to clear it. The woman had on a wedding band and was sitting in her husband's lap. It didn't matter that she was the prettiest woman I'd seen since my wife passed years ago. It didn't matter that she had the sexiest voice I'd ever heard. It didn't matter that I'd found a woman who made my heart thump around in my chest.

All that mattered was the ring on her finger and the

fact that she could never be mine.

FOUR YEARS AGO

I pulled into the parking lot and shut off my motorcycle as I smiled at the young woman walking my way.

"I told you that you'd fall in love with it, didn't I?"

"Hey there, Sis. What's up?"

"My blood pressure. We finally got Pop to try the new computer system, and within five minutes, he had it frozen. Then he got pissed off and knocked the monitor off the desk and cracked the damn thing. I'm waiting on Preacher to call and talk Pop off the ledge before he walks me through trying to get the system back online. I think Soda snuck off somewhere to have a stiff drink."

"Having Pop use a computer is like trying to teach a T-Rex to roller skate, sweetheart. It's not gonna end well, and there's gonna be serious fallout and destruction in the process."

"It's not rocket science, Chef. You push this button, click this, type in a code, and poof . . . all done. Oh, but no! The man's gotta make it . . ."

I stood up and swung my leg over my bike and then put my arm around my friend's shoulder before I pulled her tight to my side. Interrupting her, I said, "Seems like the man likes change just about as much as you do, Sis."

I felt her glaring daggers at me, but I didn't dare look because if I laughed at her, she'd get even more pissed off.

"Speaking of change, I've got some to throw at you, sweetheart."

"You're really leaving town?"

"You already heard?"

"Yeah, Hook was at the house this morning having coffee with Mom and Dad. I heard them talking while I gathered up my stuff."

"Your mom doing okay?"

"Of course. Why do you ask?"

"It's polite to ask after one's parents, sweetheart."

"You and I both know it's more than that, Chef." I didn't say a word, just squeezed her a little tighter before I let her go and opened the door to the office to let her walk in front of me. "When do you leave?"

"I'll get packed this weekend and rent a trailer so I can leave on Tuesday. I've already got an apartment rented. I'll have to do an in-service next week and start teaching three weeks from now."

"I'm going to miss you, Chef."

"You planning on never talking to me again when I leave, kiddo? Just gonna drop me like a bad habit? Replace me with some other guy you talk to death in a junkyard when all he wants to do is find some peace and fucking quiet?"

"Maybe."

"Phone works both ways, and since you taught me to text, I'm sure we'll talk all the time. Maybe you can get your parents to bring you up for a visit. I hear there's some pretty scenery where I'm going."

"Why don't you just take a job at the college here?" Sis asked as she stopped in the middle of the hallway that led from the office into the parts store where Boss worked.

"I need to get out of town and start somewhere fresh, Sis. I have to find my own way."

"Yeah," Sis said softly as she stared down at her boots. "I guess I understand that."

"I expect updates on how things are going around here, though," I told her as I reached out and gently shoved her shoulder. "I know you and Soda secretly run shit, and I like to hear about all the ways you work around Pop's inability to embrace technology."

"I'll text you so much that it drives you crazy."

"So, in essence, you're saying nothing's going to change?"

"Probably. You'd miss me if I didn't bother you."

"You're not a bother, honey. Not a bother at all," I assured her. "I think if my daughter was still alive, you'd have made pretty good friends."

"You think so?"

"I think that's probably why I put up with your shit

18

because that's as close as I'll ever get to having a kid of my own again."

"Whatever."

"I'll miss you, sweetheart. You stay safe, you hear me? I don't know what I'd do if something happened to you."

"Go on a killing spree, I'm sure."

"It's been awhile since I cooked anything up, Sis. Don't give me a reason to get back in the kitchen."

1

BREA

"I'm here! The party can start now," I announced as I walked through the front door of Boss and Jenn's.

"Oh, I'm thrilled," Preacher grumbled from his seat at the dining room table where he'd set up the laptop he was rarely ever without.

"Good to see you, too, Preach. Spouting lies and bullshit, or is it your day off?"

"Woman . . ."

"You make it too easy, Preacher," Hook teased him from the bar. "We all know Brea's secretly in love with you, and that's why she teases you."

I stared at my best friend with a blank expression until he winced and looked away. His girlfriend Paula was stirring something on the stove and laughed. "That's her serial killer stare, Hook. Watch yourself now."

"Where's Sis?" Hook asked as he glanced back at the front door.

"She's riding over with Chef. He picked her up this morning, and they went shopping or something. Fuck, I don't know. I was too busy chasing that fucking puppy you brought over to our house to listen when Sis explained her plans for the day. You know that little shit doesn't just gnaw on stuff like a normal puppy? No! He eats the *inside* of your shoes. Not the shoestrings, not even the heel. No. He crawls down into the damn thing and gnaws his way out," I bitched as I dropped my purse on the shelf under the bar beside Paula's.

"I could always take him back and find him another. . ."

"Don't even, mister," I growled. "Bruce is just fine where he is, thank you very much."

"But if he's eating your shoes . . ."

"It's a puppy phase. He'll be fine."

"What she's telling you without actually saying it is that she just likes to bitch. I swear that woman's jaw flaps like a flag in the breeze, but she never really says anything," Preacher interrupted while he glared daggers at me.

"Preacher, you make me need Jesus and a Xanax, and not in that particular order," I shot back before I turned and smiled at Stamp. "What can I do to help with dinner?"

"Honey, you're strictly entertainment." Stamp laughed as he pulled me up under his arm for a side hug. "Keep giving him shit. I want to see how red Preacher's face can get before he pops a blood vessel."

"I think they were twins separated at birth," Hook added his two cents into the discussion, always one to stir the pot when Preacher and I started arguing.

"If Memaw had a boy like him, she'd have flushed him before he was too big to plug up the toilet," Boss said from the balcony above us.

"Don't you jump in and help, Boss. As my president, I will show you a certain modicum of respect, but when you side with that woman, I forget myself."

"Preacher, the way you say 'that woman' when you refer to me makes me think you might really be sweet on me after all," I teased as I walked back around the bar toward him. He saw me coming and snapped his laptop closed before he shot up out of his chair and started for the front door. "Come here and give me some sugar, sweetheart."

"I'd rather kiss Elvira right on the starfish than put my lips anywhere near that sassy fucking mouth of yours," Preacher said over his shoulder before he walked out the front door. "I'm going outside where it's peaceful. Fuck all y'all."

"Why's he gotta bring my skunk into this?" Boss asked as came down the stairs and turned toward the kitchen. "What the fuck did she ever do to him?"

"I think Brea and Preacher should start dating," Jenn added as she walked into the room right behind Boss. "Imagine the fireworks they'd have in bed."

"I'd stab that man in the chest with a screwdriver if he got anywhere near my bedroom," I grumbled.

"That was oddly specific," Paula whispered with one eyebrow raised. "Have you been thinking about that for a while?"

"It would be harder than you think to get the screwdriver in there, Brea. You might want to consider other options," Frankie, Paula's best friend, added from her barstool. "I'd go with the ice pick."

"Who even has those anymore?" Stamp asked as he shook his head. Jenn pulled out a drawer and rifled around in it before she brandished a wooden-handled ice pick. I noticed that she was finally rid of the cast she'd been wearing since the incident in her yard, and I smiled, knowing she must be happy to be able to at least use one hand now. Stamp jerked me back to the conversation when he laughed and said, "Of course Cool Cat has one. She's got *all* the good kitchen gadgets. If I didn't know better, I'd think she was having an affair with the Amazon delivery guy."

"You're going to tease the woman while you're standing in her kitchen wearing a frilly apron, and she's holding an ice pick?" Boss asked.

"If you only knew what those aprons have seen, man," I teased Stamp, and he glanced down at the apron he had on and up at Boss before looking over at Jenn. "Don't worry. I washed them."

"Eww!" His face made it clear that he'd finally clued in to what I was implying.

"If you don't need me in here, I'm going to go work in the big kitchen for a while," I told our group. "We've got that big event this weekend, and I want to make sure I've got everything on the list so I don't have to stop and do a grocery run in the middle of cooking."

"I'll come with you," Jenn offered before she tiptoed up and kissed Boss. I saw Paula do the same with Hook just as Frankie spun her barstool around and hopped down.

The four of us walked through Jenn's kitchen out into

the larger commercial kitchen attached to her house. I'd been working for her since she was attacked in her yard. She had a cast on one arm and a splint with hardware sticking out on the other. There was no way she could cook and clean, so Boss had asked me to step in and help her while she was recovering. I was enjoying it, and couldn't imagine what I'd do with all my time once she was back in action.

Frankie and Paula sat down on the stools that Jenn kept out there. I walked over to one of the shelves beside the walk-in refrigerator and pulled the day planner and recipe binder down. I put them on the wide metal workbench before I reached over and pulled the laptop toward me from its space by the wall charger. I listened to the girls' chatter while I waited for it to go through the opening screens and then I navigated around to find the software Jenn used to keep track of her recipes and ingredients.

"Okay, I can't take it anymore. I have to ask," I heard Frankie say before she got up and pushed the kitchen door closed. "What's the deal with Sis and Chef? Are they dating?"

"No," I scoffed. "Chef is not dating my daughter."

I didn't want to analyze how I felt about the thought of Chef dating *anyone* but most especially, my little girl.

"Chef's holding out for someone else," Paula said knowingly. "You've got the right gene pool, but the wrong generation."

"My mom's not dating Chef either," I joked.

"That just leaves you then," Frankie said with a grin. "You go, girl."

"I'm not dating Chef or anyone else for that matter. I've been in love, married, and lived through a lot of loss . . . I've got the t-shirt and therapy bills to prove it."

"Chef's got that in common with you, doesn't he?" Jenn asked softly. "I've seen the way he watches you, Brea. Surely, you've noticed."

"I've known all these guys for years, ladies. There's nothing between me and any of them, and there's never going to be. Although I will admit they're some nice eye candy, I don't have the time or the energy to date. And I'm not interested anyway."

"She did not deny that Chef watches her, though. Did you hear that?" Paula teased. "I've seen you scoping him out, too, woman. Don't even try to deny it."

"Have you seen the man, Paula? You can't help but look at him. When he's in the room, he takes up 90% of it because of his sheer size. I haven't been scoping him out; he just blocks out the sun, and I'm trying to see around him."

"Ah, deflection. Good play," Frankie said from her seat across from me. "Let's move right into denial next, shall we?"

"Why are you here again?"

"There's *more* deflection," Jenn agreed. "Moving on to irritation and possibly picking a fight to turn the conversation to something else."

"Am I gonna get billed for this impromptu intervention, or is the first one a freebie?" I grumbled before I turned around to double check the amount of flour in the storage bin.

"You were pretty emotional when he got shot. It freaked you out."

"Well, Paula, I tend to freak out when anyone gets shot or kidnapped. Somehow, that's in my nature. I also react badly when someone is stabbed or attacked with a knife." I motioned toward Jenn and watched Paula grimace. "Did you freak out when that happened to her?" Paula nodded, and after a few seconds, I continued, "Ladies, there are circumstances at play here that you might not understand. I'm not sure you want to dive into that pool."

Frankie just wouldn't let it go. "When you look at him, it's like watching Paula look at Hook or Jenn look at Boss. It's not hard to see how you feel about him, Brea. We know there's history there."

"I'll admit, there's something about Chef that draws me to him. We've been friends for a few years now, and about a year after my husband passed away, things started to feel different between us. But, and this is a but big enough to fit in with the Kardashians, I am not ever going to act on these new feelings. There isn't enough time or Kleenex to get into all the reasons I can't - *won't* - date one of the guys, or any man for that matter."

"Is it because he's an ex-con?" Frankie asked softly. "It's not a secret that all of them are, so I'm not giving anything away here, right?"

I got a pain in my forehead from how hard my eyes rolled at Frankie's question. I seriously wondered how in the world I'd gotten caught up in this hen party. This exact scenario was why I was *not* a fan of having a gaggle of female friends around and the reason I felt more comfortable surrounded by the guys. I was not one for sharing my feelings or my demons either, for that matter. Women always expected you to spill every detail.

"I don't know why exactly Chef went to prison, but I know he had a wife and daughter and they're dead now. That's what I meant when I said he got the t-shirt too. He knows what it's like to lose a spouse. Other than Boss, Chef might be the one you have the most in common with out of the guys," Paula pointed out. "What I don't understand is why you won't let your guard down with one of the guys you know best."

Jenn answered with an assumption of her own, "Maybe she can't separate it, and that's why she can't ever see love as a possibility with one of them."

"Jesus H. Christ. I didn't say I can't love one of them. I love all of them, and I am *in* love with Chef and can't do anything about it, okay? I just can't. I can't love someone and lose them again. Chef getting shot fucking drove that point home with me. No amount of harping from you ladies is going to make it any easier. If anything, you should offer some support and help me get past the fact that I can't ever be with the man I love! Shit!" I took a deep breath and blew it out before I put my hands up and stepped back from the counter. "Preacher had the right idea. I fucking need some air!"

I stormed over to the door and flung it open before I said something I'd regret. As I walked through the kitchen, I noticed that my daughter had arrived. I nodded in her direction as I passed, but she didn't say a word. She had a

CHEF

lifetime of experience gauging my moods, and she knew that right now was not the time for a chat.

Now, as long as no one else got in my way, I'd go outside and take a minute before I came back refreshed and ready to start this evening over.

CHEF

"Lift up just a hair more," Boss ordered from above me on the ladder. I did as he requested, grunting with the effort, until Boss said, "That's good right there. Thanks, Chef."

Hook laughed from where he was casually leaning against the wall watching us work and commented, "You've got the shelf up there now, but how are you going to get shit up and down off that shelf without calling Too Tall over for help?"

"This is one of those women things, man. Once I get everything up there, she's probably not ever going to miss it. She doesn't want to throw the shit away even though she all but admitted that she hasn't looked in these boxes since before she moved to Texas."

"Why the fuck did she bring them with her if she doesn't even know what's in them?" I asked as I looked at the hanging shelf I'd held while Boss attached the four corners.

"Hell, I don't know what's in there; I just know that she asked me to find a safe place for them where she wouldn't be tripping over them all the time. Can you hand them up?"

28

Hook pushed away from the wall and picked up one of the plastic tubs. He held it up until Boss could grab it and slide it over toward the middle of the shelf. In just a minute or two, we got all the tubs situated up against the ceiling of the garage. I leaned up against the trailer while Boss stepped down off the ladder and started folding it up.

I heard a noise over my shoulder and realized it was Brea's muffled voice. I walked a little closer to the door that led into Jenn's commercial kitchen, and without any remorse, I eavesdropped on the women.

"What are they saying in there?" Hook whispered as he stepped up to stand beside me, both of us leaning against the door now.

"They're having an intervention? Like on TV? What's that about?"

"When she looks at *who*?" Hook whispered. His eyes went wide and his mouth dropped when he heard the same thing I did. "When she looks at *you*?"

"What the fuck are we doing?" Boss whispered from behind us.

"Shh!" Hook and I hushed him at the same time.

I stepped back from the door and stared at it as if it were about to spontaneously combust. Hook stepped in front of me and I looked up to see that he was grinning from ear to ear.

"She's in love with you."

"Who?" Boss asked.

"Brea just admitted she's in love with Chef and then got so pissed that she stormed out. Now the girls are all aflutter about true love," Hook explained.

Boss laughed and said, "It's about goddamn time. Watching the two of them give each other goo-goo eyes when the other wasn't looking was getting old. They've been doing that shit for years."

"I know, right?" Hook agreed.

"She's not happy about it."

"Well, Chef, she does have a point. She loved her husband, and it damn near killed her when he died. Then, before shit even happened between the two of you, you got yourself shot. Might have managed to make the woman a little skittish, you think?"

"Hook's got a point," Boss agreed.

Hook picked up again with, "Life's not set in stone. Shit can happen to anyone. You can bump your head and throw a clot or something and die before you realize you've even stumbled. Or you can live until you're that old guy saying inappropriate shit to the nurses when they bring you your Jell-O. Not sure she's willing to stick her neck out at this point and take a risk again."

"I'm not a risk," I argued. "That was a one-time thing."

Boss and Hook just stared at me.

"Okay, so I'll try not to get shot at again. If I do, I'll try to duck a little quicker."

"This puts me in a rough spot," Hook admitted. "She's my girl. She always will be. You're my brother. Seeing the two of you together could be awesome. Dealing with the two of you if shit goes south would not be awesome."

"She's one hell of a stubborn woman," Boss pointed out unnecessarily. "She's an immovable force, man. I don't know how you would ever change her mind."

"A steady drip of water can carve a hole in stone if given enough time, Boss. I've just got to figure out how to get close enough to turn on the tap."

2

BREA

"You're such a sweetheart," I murmured to the little goat who was currently trying to eat the sleeve of my hoodie. There was another one trying to poke his head into the pocket and yet another chewing on my shoelace. I'd heard Jenn talk about going out to sit with the goats when she was having a rough day, and honestly, I'd thought she sounded mental. Now that I'd tried it, I'd probably end up out here for a dose of serotonin every time I came over. "Don't tell Hook I said that, or I'll end up with a herd of you guys at my house."

"What will you offer in exchange for my silence?"

My entire body jolted, and I bumped my head on the wall behind me as I let out an ear-piercing scream.

"Hello there." Chef laughed from just outside the stall door.

"For such a big man, it's disturbing just how quiet you can be."

Chef opened the short door and came inside as he asked, "You didn't realize I'm a ninja?"

I laughed and reached up to make sure my face was dry, hoping that Chef couldn't tell I'd been crying. I'd stormed out of the house mad as a wet hen, but by the time I got out to the barn, that had worn off and the waterworks had started. I wasn't sure if I was crying because I was mad at the girls for pushing me too far, or if I was crying because I'd finally admitted that I wanted something I could never have.

Maybe it was a little bit of both. Right now, the reason for at least some of those tears was crouching down in front of me being attacked by the cute goats I'd befriended.

"Come here, Pickle," Chef said as he reached out and took my hands. He stood and pulled me up with him, and before I knew what was going on, he had me in a tight hug against his broad chest. "What's got you upset?"

"I'm not upset," I argued as I tried to push myself back and get some space between us.

"Since when did you start lying?"

"I'm not lying either!" I pushed again, but he held me close. He wasn't squeezing me with any kind of force, but his arms were so long that he had them wrapped all the way around me. I couldn't seem to get out of his embrace.

"Hush," Chef said in that sexy, deep voice of his, and damned if I didn't just instantly calm down. I didn't mean to, but for some reason, when he used that tone, I couldn't help but do what he asked. I'd have to explore that issue later. Right now, I needed to get away before I burst into tears again. Chef moved one of his hands slowly up my back until his fingers were in the hair at the back of my head. As he held me to his chest, he started to gently massage the muscles at the base of my skull with his thumb while his fingers massaged my scalp. It was all I could do to hold in a moan of ecstasy at just how good that felt. "You're all worked up about something. What's going on?"

"Nothing's wrong, I'm just having a moment. I needed some time alone."

"You cry when nothing's wrong? What's that about?"

Chef's fingers were working on my head, and I felt my entire body start to relax. It felt so good to have his arms around me, but the hand in my hair was such an added bonus. It had been so long since someone held me like this that I felt my eyes start to fill up again with the emotion of it all. I didn't know where the tears were coming from today, but I'd had about enough of this shit. It was completely unlike me.

"I'm not crying," I huffed and immediately ruined my argument with a sniff followed by a sob I didn't stifle in time.

Chef held me a little tighter for a second and then tugged my head back by the hair he was holding and stared down into my face. He leaned forward, and I thought he was going to kiss me, but instead, he kissed the apples of my cheeks where the tears had run down my face. I was trapped again, one hand holding me against him and the other holding my head back, but I didn't mind. It felt comfortable somehow. It also felt so damn good that my entire body was reacting and not in a sweet way. Every inch of my body that was touching him was on fire right now. I wanted to turn my head and catch his lips with mine.

"Don't lie to me, Pickle," Chef whispered as he softly rained kisses all over my cheeks. "Liars get punished. Good girls that tell the truth get rewarded."

"Huh?" I asked, confused now, but overwhelmed by

the fact that his mouth was kissing ever closer to mine.

Right before he kissed the corner of my lips, he whispered, "You heard me, sugar. What am I gonna do with you?"

"Do with me?" I squeaked out.

"There are so many things I want to do to you and do with you, but right now is not the time, and this is not the place," Chef murmured with his lips just barely touching mine. I could feel his warm breath on my lips as he spoke. Every word he said felt like he was softly nibbling at my mouth. "What can I do to make you feel better?"

"Better?" All of a sudden, I couldn't speak in full sentences or even form a coherent thought. Not only was this big man a fucking ninja, but he was some sort of sensual sex god too. I was caught in his spell, and I had no control over my brain or body anymore.

"Maybe this," Chef whispered before he pressed his lips to mine. He used the hand in my hair to angle my head just the way he wanted it before he deepened the kiss. Without even realizing what I was about to do, I kissed him back. I opened my mouth just a bit when I felt his tongue touch my lips and then the arm around my back crushed me to him, and he touched his tongue to mine.

It could have been just a minute, or it could have been an hour. I had no concept of time while his lips were on mine. I moaned at the loss when he pulled his head back a fraction and groaned.

"I've been dying to do that, Pickle, and I'm gonna do it again soon. Right now, though, there's a fucking herd of women walking out here to make sure you're okay. I don't want them all up in our business, so I'm gonna let you go. But I want you to know that we're not finished by a long shot, sweetheart. I've had a taste now, and I'll be thinking about it until the next time I get one. Will you?"

"I will," I said on an exhale, my words barely louder than a sigh.

I hadn't realized my feet weren't touching the ground until Chef set me back down. My knees were weak. He held me upright for a second until I had my balance, then let me go and took a step back. He reached out and ran his thumb across my swollen lips as he smiled.

"I'll see you back at the house for dinner, Pickle," Chef whispered before he gave me one last, quick kiss on the lips.

"Okay," I whispered back just as I heard Jenn's voice outside the barn door.

Chef was out of the stall and across the barn in a blink. I watched him walk into the fenced area where the animals roamed during the day just as I heard the main barn door open and the chattering women start down the aisle.

I reached up and touched my lips as I stared at the door that Chef had disappeared through, wondering what in the hell had just happened.

I'd just been put in a trance by a 6'6" man who crept in silent as a ninja, held me so tight yet he could sweep me off my feet without me even knowing and could make love to my mouth with his so well that every nerve in my body was on fire, begging for more.

"Brea? Are you okay?" Paula asked as she stared at me over the stall door. Jenn's face appeared on one side of Paula's and Frankie's on the other. It looked like there were floating heads talking to me: a brunette, a blonde, and a redhead. All three of them were staring at me like they were afraid I was about to combust. "What's wrong?"

I still had my hand over my lips and eyed the door Chef had walked through before I turned my attention back to the girls.

"I think I just had an out of body experience or a hallucination or something," I admitted.

"Why are your lips puffy? Have you been crying?" Frankie asked as she opened the stall door to come inside. She reached for my hand and held it in hers as she put her fingers on my wrist. "Your face is flushed, and your pulse is racing. Are you feeling okay?"

"I'm fine," I whispered.

"You look like you just saw a ghost," Paula said in a soft voice. "Are you sure you're okay?"

"I know what's wrong with her," Jenn crowed. "Boss mauled me in the hallway one morning, and when he let me go, I walked into the bathroom and saw myself in the mirror. I looked *just like that*. Brea's surfing the hot man high right now."

"Those must have been some naughty thoughts because she's in here alone," Paula pointed out. "I see it, though. I'm pretty sure I look like that when Hook gets done with me sometimes."

"Who else wasn't in the house when we walked outside?" Frankie asked the girls.

"Preacher was on the front porch with Cap, Santa, and Kitty. Bug, Hook, and Boss were sitting at the bar talking to Stamp. That just leaves . . ."

"Chef!" Frankie and Jenn said in unison.

"Holy shit! Brea got roughed up in the barn by Chef!" Paula exclaimed as she clapped her hands excitedly.

Frankie laughed before she said, "That sounds like a sexy version of Clue."

"Look at her blushing," Jenn teased. "Oh wow. She went from white as a sheet to blushing like a virgin on her wedding night!"

"Does that still happen? The virgin thing?" Paula asked off-handedly, and I prayed that would take the focus off me.

"Not likely in this day and age, although I'm sure there are a few exceptions," Frankie put in her two cents even though she was still staring at me with her fingers on the pulse at my wrist. I realized I wasn't going to get my reprieve when Frankie said, "So, Chef came out to the barn, got you alone, and kissed you senseless? You're still not talking, so I guess it was that good, huh?"

"Damn, girl," Paula said cheerfully. "If he can do that in just a few minutes with his lips on yours, can you imagine if he had all night, naked in a bed somewhere? Jeez."

"I can't," I whispered. I didn't know if I was telling

them I couldn't imagine what he could do or if I was trying to remind myself that nothing could happen with Chef. I shook my head and jerked my hand away from Frankie's, pulling together my resolve and finding the steel in my spine before I said, "It's not gonna happen. I'm not dealing with this shit, and this is not going anywhere with Chef. I'm going to tell him that just as soon as I can get him alone."

"I have a feeling that the next time the two of you are alone, there won't be a whole lot of talking going on," Jenn mused. "Maybe a whole lot of moaning and grunting, most likely a scream or two, but not much talking."

The women laughed, but I didn't. I had a feeling Jenn was right, so I'd have to make sure I wasn't ever alone with that man.

Chef was dangerous, and those lips of his should be outlawed. So should that voice. And his hands . . . I shook my head again to clear it, wondering how in the hell the man had kissed me stupid in just a few minutes.

I'd said it to Preacher earlier, but that was a joke. Now I *really* needed Jesus and a Xanax.

"Okay, you guys. Brea helped me with all of your results, and we're ready to have the big reveal!" Jenn announced excitedly from her seat at the table next to Boss. "She's been taking care of the computer tasks since I've been without hands for a while, and we've gotten your exact makeup."

"Mutts. We're all mutts," Hook announced. "See?

CHEF

There ya go. You didn't even have to pay all that money or log in to shit. That's what it's going to say."

"You'd be surprised, big guy," I told him as I pulled up his account on my laptop. "Now, we've taken great pains to make all of you anonymous on this site. We set up an email account for each of you and used it as your login, and we didn't list your names anywhere. We can look at your percentages and be done with it, or I can give each of you your information and you can see if you have any relatives out there and dig into your family tree."

"We'll show up on their profiles, though, right?"

"You will show up on other's trees, and you'll be listed as whatever relation you are to them, but they won't have your name. If you come from a small family, they'll be able to figure out who you are because of your connection to them, but if you've got a pretty big family with lots of cousins or whatever and not all of them have taken the test yet, you'll still be mostly anonymous."

"Yeah, sure, Mouth. Anonymous. They've got our DNA now. There's no anonymity left for any of us," Preacher whined.

"At some point, I'm going to just shoot you," Captain growled. "I'll just pull out my gun and fucking shoot you."

"Stop calling me Mouth, *Jude*, or I'll start referring to you as Micropenis," I snapped at Preacher.

"I'll prove to you that there's nothing micro about it," Preacher threatened as he stood up and started unbuckling his belt.

"Sit your ass down," Chef boomed, and Preacher fell back down into his chair with a thump. Chef cleared his throat as every head at the table turned his way. "Nobody wants to see that scrawny dick of yours."

Hook and Boss started chuckling, but everyone else at the table was still stunned at the tone Chef had used when he barked at Preacher. I glanced over at Jenn and saw that she had her lips pulled in between her teeth to hold back her smile, but Paula and Frankie were sporting giant grins. I was surrounded by assholes that I'd formerly referred to as friends.

I needed a new circle of people to hang out with and fast.

"I'm Italian. That's what this thing is going to say. Big neon letters that scream, 'He's 100% Italian stallion and there's no doubt about it!'" Stamp boasted as I rolled my eyes.

"We'll start with Mr. Mafia then," I said with a laugh. I typed in his login information and waited on the page to load. "84% Italian, 11% German, 4% from England, and 1% Other. Mostly Italian, but not quite as pristine as you thought, buddy."

"I call bullshit. Look at me. Do you see any German?"

"DNA doesn't lie. It's probably the only part of you that can't," Hook told our friend with a laugh. "I'm next, Brea!"

I opened another tab on my browser and logged in as Hook. "Well, you were right about your being a mutt. English, Scottish, Irish, Icelandic, Norwegian, and German."

"You are the whitest man I've ever met, hands down," Chef teased Hook.

"Don't get too cocky, big guy," I interrupted. My breath caught when Chef's deep brown eyes shot my way and studied me. I tried to cover my reaction by opening another tab and logging in as Chef. "Okay, Mr. Green . . . "

"In the barn with a candlestick," Paula blurted and then slapped her hand over her mouth. Frankie and Jenn burst out laughing

"More like a lead pipe," Jenn yelled before she threw her head back and cackled.

Frankie chimed in with, "As long as a rope!"

I put my elbow up on the table and leaned my head forward so I could rub my forehead while I tried to calm down. It would be hard to bury three bodies at once, so I'd need to step back and make some plans to take them out one at a time. Or I could see about renting a backhoe. That might be a better plan anyway.

"Are they drunk?" Preacher asked.

"I think they've been eating Paula's special candy," Stamp answered him.

My eyes went straight to Chef. He was leaning back in his chair with his big arms crossed over his chest and a knowing grin on his face. I felt my face get hot and knew I was blushing again. I had to get that shit lined out. I usually had a poker face that no one could read. Apparently, three minutes with Chef had sucked that ability right out of me.

"Moving on!" I belted as I glared at each woman in turn. They at least had the good sense to look ashamed, but it was too little too late. I was still plotting their deaths. "Chef, you're 88% African, and your DNA shows you come from a region that includes Angola, Zambia, and the Congo. The rest is 21% French and 1% other."

"Merci, mon amour," Chef said as he nodded his head in my direction. "Tu es belle chérie."

"Holy shit. She tells you your DNA, and you suddenly know the language?" Bug asked, amazed.

"My granny and grandpa spoke Cajun French," Chef explained. "I don't remember everything, just the important stuff."

I'd taken Spanish in high school, so the only French words I knew, I'd learned from music and movies. However, I knew enough to realize he'd called me his love right here in a room full of our friends.

I'd need to dig a much deeper hole, and instead of killing my friends and burying them, I could just crawl down there myself. That might be the only way to escape that predatory look in the man's eyes.

Having known Chef for a few years now, I understood that look. It meant that there wasn't a hole deep enough or a place far enough to hide. He'd set his mind to something, and he was even more stubborn than I was.

I was well and truly screwed. No pun intended.

3

CHEF

"Jesus, it'd be easier to just go out and bench press a fucking house," Hook complained from the mat beside me. "You keep adding to that shit, and they're gonna run out of weights."

"Whatever."

"Let me go get those two guys that just came in. I can see if they'll perch on the ends of the bar so you can max out."

"Are you gonna spot me or not?"

"How the fuck do you think I can spot you? I can't lift half that weight. Damn," Hook grumbled as he stepped up and stood above my head. I reached up and settled my hands on the bar and pushed up to begin. I noticed that Hook had his phone out and wasn't even paying attention to me. "Did you know that with the weight you've got on there now, you could be lifting three beer kegs? Or five toilets? Damn. Fifty gallons of paint!"

"You gonna play on your phone and spout bullshit," I grunted with effort as I pushed the bar up and then let it come down again. "Or are you gonna spot me, fucker?"

"I got it out to take pictures of that chick they told us to look for. She's over on the treadmill, walking at a snail's pace," Hook explained as he put his phone back in his pocket. "Sloths move faster when they're feeling lazy than she does when she's working out."

"What the fuck's she doing here then?" I grunted through three more lifts before Hook helped me settle the bar in the grooves so I could rest before my next round.

"She's following a guy back into the office. I got a picture of her walking in. We'll stay here until she walks out."

Once we'd finished our bench presses, we moved over to a different machine to work on our shoulders. After I adjusted the weights, I stepped under the machine and reached up to grab the bar that was hanging above my head. I'd just finished my first set of ten when Hook started in on me.

"So, Brea, huh?"

"Yep."

"You're well aware she's my best friend, right?"

"Yep."

"I guess this is where I ask what your intentions are with my girl," Hook admitted. He seemed a little uncomfortable, but I had to give him credit for looking out for his friend. Brea didn't have any men in her life other than our group, so Hook was willing to step up and be the man to watch out for her in this case. "You've got an uphill battle ahead of you, and I want to make sure you've got the sticking power, you know?"

"What are my intentions?" I ground out as I pulled the bar down behind my head and held it there for a few seconds while I took a few deep breaths.

"And can you stick it out? She's fucking stubborn, man. You know that."

"I'm gonna give her romance until she begs me to fuck her senseless and then I'll keep her in an orgasm stupor long enough to drag her in front of a preacher. Once her last name is Green, I'm going to spend the rest of my days on earth keeping her happy, no matter what I've got to do to get her there." I watched Hook's eyebrows raise incrementally the longer I talked until his eyes were so wide, I could see the whites all around them. His eyebrows were damn near touching his hairline. "You look shocked. I've been in love with her since the first time she spoke to me. I left town to get away from the one woman I could never have. I can have her now, and I will. You wanted me to lie or something?"

"Well, no. I didn't need all those details about shit though," Hook admitted. "You could have just said I want to marry her."

I held the bar and let it raise slowly until the weight was settled and then took my hands down. While I shook out my arms and did a few stretches, I told him, "Fine. I'm gonna marry her. Is that better? There's the woman. She's carrying a bag now."

"She wasn't carrying anything when she went back to the office," Hook said as he pulled his phone out and discreetly took a video of Officer Hannigan walking out of the gym with a heavy bag hanging from one hand. "What do you think is in that bag?"

"Something that weighs a few pounds. Look how it's straining the handles."

"Are we finished here?" Hook asked me. "I'll get this information to Boss. I know Sin's got a tail on that chick, so we're free and clear now."

"Yeah, I'm picking up Sis for lunch. Want to join us?"

"I'm going home to shower and kiss on my woman. Meet you at the shop in two hours?"

"Will do. I've got an errand to run on my way home. Two hours will give me plenty of time."

"Something to do with Brea?"

"I was thinking of taking her flowers. What do you suggest?"

"Nah, man. She can kill a plant just by standing near it. Take her something she likes, something she can use. Something practical."

"I don't want practical, man, I want some romantic win her heart bullshit."

"Yeah, that sounds perfect. Tell her that's what you're giving her and use those exact words. I'll be able to hear her front door slam all the way over at my place."

"Man, fuck you."

"You'll figure it out."

I had no idea what in the world to get Brea other than flowers, and Hook blew that out of the water. I couldn't go to Jenn or Paula because they'd probably tell Brea every word I said, and I didn't know Frankie well enough to call her for advice.

However, a few weeks back, I'd met the woman that owned Blossoms flower shop. I'd helped cover the store for the Infidels while they were trying to figure out who was trying to get Jackie, the owner and Executioner's future mother-in-law, to pay them protection money to keep her store and family safe.

The shit going on with Jackie's family had come to a head a few days ago, and I'd been busy helping the men of AIMC with that, so I hadn't spoken to Brea in damn near a week. I'd worried that she might be shoring up her defenses without any contact with me but realized that if she was home stewing over what she was going to say to me, she'd at least be thinking of our stolen moments in the barn. Any thoughts were good thoughts at this point. At least I was on her mind somehow.

I pulled up in front of Blossoms and was shocked to see Captain's bike parked out front. I pulled even with his motorcycle and backed mine in so I could park beside him, wondering what in the hell he had going on that required flowers. He was a good friend of mine, but he kept his shit pretty close to the vest. He might be seeing someone on the sly and just not ready or willing to bring his latest piece around our club family.

When I walked in, my question was answered almost instantly. Cap was leaning forward with his elbows on the counter, laughing with Jackie about something. The two of them looked pretty fucking cozy together, and I thought that might be a good thing. The woman had been dealt a shit hand by her ex, and Cap was just the kind of man to bring some good into her life.

I had a feeling that the new prospect Executioner had

brought in a few weeks ago might have a problem with that, considering how he'd been glued to Jackie's side almost every time I'd seen them together lately.

Either way, Jackie's love life was none of my business. I needed to focus on my own goal. Brea was going to be a hard nut to crack, but I think I'd found the perfect woman to help me.

"Hi, Chef," Jackie greeted me as I approached the counter. Cap nodded in my direction but didn't stand up from his seat at the counter. "What can I do for you today, sir?"

"Well, I need to figure out what to send a woman that's not into flowers."

"And you thought coming to a flower shop was the way to get that done?" Cap teased.

"Nah, I thought Ms. Jackie here might be able to help me without blabbing my shit to the rest of that crazy coven of women."

"Crazy coven?"

"You get those women together, and it messes with the universe. You should hear them cackling together when no one's around to hear what they're talking about. I've thought about asking Preacher to bug Jenn's kitchen, but I figured Boss might have a problem with that."

"Or," Captain pushed himself up to stand before he continued, "there might just be a recording of whatever kinky shit they get up to when they're alone."

"There's that too," I grumbled.

"You don't want to know what the women talk about when men aren't around, Chef. Some of it might make you laugh, but some things they say very well might hurt your fragile egos too."

"Jackie might have a point," Captain agreed. "So, what's this idea you've got? I've known Brea for a time. I might be able to help you."

"I want to send her some of her favorite things. She doesn't do flowers. It's a little early yet to buy her diamonds . . ."

"Yet?" Cap interrupted. "Damn. It's about time you got your head out of your ass and staked your claim. Good job, brother."

I shook my head with a sigh and looked back at Jackie with a smile, "What do you think of that idea?"

"I think it sounds great. Is this a one-time thing, or do you want to spread out the gifts and keep her thinking about you?"

"Oh, Jackie, you're good," Cap said softly. "I'll have to keep that idea in my arsenal for the future."

"Can you get the stuff for me and dress it up a little bit? Do you have someone who can deliver it to her?"

"We have a guy we use if you're willing to pay his fee."

"I'm willing. Maybe start sending her little things, one at a time, every other day."

"That's gonna cost you, man," Captain pointed out.

I shrugged.

"He's willing to put in the effort, fork out the money, and do something nice for her. She'll appreciate that, I think. I've met Brea. She's got a good head on her shoulders. She and I made plans to go have coffee together soon."

"Can you keep this a secret for me?"

"Of course. Business is business, right?" She smiled brightly and slid a small pad of paper and a pen across the counter toward me. "Give me a list, and I'll have the first gift delivered to her this afternoon."

"You'll also want to fork over your credit card, brother," Cap told me with a laugh. "This shit's gonna get expensive."

I pulled my wallet out of my pocket and took a few bills out. I slid them across the counter toward Jackie and her eyes got wide. "Let's say Monday, Wednesday, Friday for the next two weeks. I can tell you where she'll be on those days and when, I think. If you run out of money, let me know, and I'll bring you more cash. Will you give the delivery guy a decent tip for me?"

"Yes, of course," Jackie agreed. "I thought you didn't want jewelry, Chef. That's an awful lot of money."

"You've got to go buy the stuff and jazz it up. You'll charge me for your time and effort, the delivery guy's fee and tip, and we should be square, right?"

"I can do that." Jackie smiled. "Now, let's get to work

on your list."

BREA

"Pop, you're making me stir crazy with your pacing," I told my old friend. "Sit a spell, and let me get your house in order."

"I don't think it's part of your job description to come over here and mess with my shit, little lady."

"I've been coming over to your house twice a week for years, and yet, you're still bitching about me *messing with your shit*. That bluster got old after year one, old man."

"You're too sassy for your own good. You know that, right?" Pop sat down in one of the kitchen chairs with a huff.

"But you love me, and that's all that matters," I told him as I leaned down to kiss him on the cheek. "What do you want from the grocery store next week? I'll bring everything Monday morning when I come out."

"No sense in telling you what I want. You'll buy what you think I need to eat and leave all the good stuff on the shelves. Should have never let you read that shit the doctor sent home with me."

"You think I wouldn't just *know* that a man who suffered a massive heart attack and just recently released from rehab after getting shot and having open heart surgery shouldn't have bacon with every meal? Really?"

"Like I said, sassy."

"I bought you turkey bacon."

"What part of a pig did that shit come from, Brea? Tell me. Better yet, let's fucking go find a pig, and you can show me the exact spot where they get that turkey bacon. There must be some new breed of pig, and I want to get a good look at it."

"It tastes just the same, Pop."

"Like hell it does," Pop grumbled. "I could go to the damn store on my own, you know? Why don't I just do that?"

"That's one hell of a way to waste your money. I'd just have to throw all that shit out when I come over next week."

"Little girl, I'll spank your ass. Don't think I won't."

I laughed as I carried the hamper out into the laundry room. The man was all bluster, and we both knew it. I had just closed the lid for the machine to start when I heard the doorbell. I leaned back so I could look across the kitchen and living room to the front door. There was a man standing there holding a box in his hand.

"Pop? Where'd you go?" I yelled, wondering how in the world a damn near 80-year-old man could move that fast. When he didn't answer, I started for the door. I opened the screen and smiled, "Can I help you?"

"Delivery for Brea," the man announced pleasantly.

"Really?" I asked as I reached out and took the box. "Let me get you a tip."

"It's taken care of already, ma'am. Have a great day!" The guy turned and walked down the steps toward his car before I could say anything else. I stood there wondering just where the hell Pop had snuck off to before I pulled the screen door shut and headed back to the kitchen. As I walked, I studied the box.

It was small, taped closed, and didn't have any markings on the outside. I was half afraid to open it. I'd watched way too many episodes of Criminal Minds, apparently, because I could just imagine what might be inside the box.

"Shit," I whispered, my curiosity getting the better of me. I pulled a knife out of the block on the counter and slit the tape. I opened the box and found yellow tissue paper. No blood or anything gory, so I felt a little better about it, at least. Once I folded the tissue paper back, I found a coffee mug.

I pulled it out and saw a cactus on the side and beside it in bold font, it read MOOD. I smiled, knowing that whoever sent the gift must know me well. I guessed, considering his disappearing act, it had to be Pop. He'd just been afraid he'd ruin the surprise. When I looked inside the mug, I saw a small envelope. I set the mug down to read the enclosed card.

Don't get all prickly, just enjoy your coffee and think of me.

Marques

"What the hell?" I whispered as I stared at the bold handwriting.

I'd kept myself busier than usual trying to keep my mind off the man. Every time my thoughts strayed to Chef or our little meeting in the barn, I'd jump up from my chair and do something productive around the house. In the last five days, I'd barely gotten a full night's sleep, hadn't eaten an entire plate of food, and was running on fumes because all I'd done lately was clean and reorganize every closet, drawer, and surface of my entire house.

Twice.

And now it looked like it was time to get started on Pop's.

4

CHEF

"Do you think you've got the concept now, Brandon?"

The guy I'd been tutoring for the last three months had a final tomorrow. If I could just convince him to relax, he'd ace the damn thing. If he walked into that room wound up as tight as he was right now, he'd fail it before he ever got started.

"Dr. Green, I'm not sure. I think I do, but I might . . ."

"Listen, bro," I said, taking myself out of teacher mode and sliding back into a regular guy with some life experience under my belt. "You know this shit like the back of your hand. Hell, at this point you could probably teach me a thing or two. You need to step away from the books for tonight. Hang out with some friends or turn on your Xbox for a while. Eat some good food, go to sleep at a decent hour, wake up and have a healthy breakfast, and then go kill it."

"Maybe I should just . . ."

I heard my front door open but didn't turn around. This kid needed something, and my focus was on him right now.

"Your assignment tonight is to put down the damn book, Brandon. Your parents hired me to help you, and this is me helping you. Get out of your head, chill for a few hours, and rock that shit tomorrow. You feel me?"

"I guess I could play Xbox if I can find anyone I know online."

"Text me your gamer tag, and I'll find you. Tonight at 7:00. That's in two hours. We'll blow some shit up, kill a few zombies, and just chill. That's your homework."

"Thanks, Dr. Green. I think I'm gonna go grab some food and drive around for a while, but I'll be back at 7:00."

"That's it, my man. Just step away. You got this shit. I'll talk to you online later."

"Later."

I hit the button to end the video chat and then disconnected my camera and put it in the drawer at my side. I spun my chair around and saw Bug and Kitty sitting on my couch with beers in hand.

"I sure as hell never had a teacher tell me to dick around before a big test," Bug complained.

"The kid was failing the class when we started, and he's gotta be in the top three now. He's got this shit down, but he's worked himself up to the point of having performance anxiety tomorrow. There is such a thing as too much studying, I swear."

"I've got my Xbox set up. I'll play with you guys tonight," Kitty offered. Bug nodded, and I knew he would be online too. "How old's this guy?"

"He's 23. Should have graduated last semester, but this class held him back."

"No wonder the kid's freaking out. Nothing like some

pressure to make your asshole pucker, am I right?" Bug asked. It was a horrible visual, but he had a point. "Let's go for a ride and grab something to eat."

"I could eat."

"You're always eating," Kitty said seriously. "I can't imagine the amount of money it takes to feed your ass. If I ate as much as you, I'd have to take up robbing people again to afford it."

"My mom raised three more just like me. Imagine that shit," I told him with a laugh. "I've got to get down there and visit her. We should take a road trip when this shit around here gets settled. I'll introduce you assholes to my family and show you what kind of cooking makes regular kids grow up to look like me and my brothers."

"How big is your dad?"

"I'd say he's about your size. Maybe a little shorter."

"I'm only 6' tall, man," Kitty grumbled. "How big's your mom?"

"Shit. She's not much more than 5'. Mom's a tiny little thing. Weighs 100 pounds soaking wet, but she can still whip our asses."

"Your brother still play ball?"

"Two of them do. One's up in New York, and the others in Chicago now."

"What about the fourth one?"

"Married with five sons. His life is fucking nuts. He

had to retire just to help his wife take care of the kids."

"Shit. Are they all your size?"

"My brothers?"

"And your nephews?"

"We're all close to the same size. My nephews are young, but I'm pretty sure they're bigger than all their friends. My daughter was a big kid growing up. She was damn near 6'1" full-grown."

I saw my friends' faces go blank when I mentioned my daughter, but I was used to that. For some reason, people didn't know what to say when I talked about her, but that didn't stop me. I still missed her every single day. That wasn't going to stop either.

As if I'd conjured up a change of subject, someone knocked on my door. Within just a second, the knob turned and Sis let herself in.

"Hey, Sis," Bug greeted her. "What's kickin' chicken?"

"Mom's in a tizzy, and I need to hide for a while." She slapped Kitty's feet so he'd put them on the floor and give her room to sit on the other end of the couch. "I just can't deal with her when she gets like this."

"Like what? What's wrong?"

"She's got her panties in a bunch about something she got in the mail today. She's over at Pop's house reorganizing his shit, and he's about to lose it. She started organizing his junk drawer and throwing things in the trash, and I thought he was going to have another freaking heart attack. When I left, he was stomping around yelling, and she was completely ignoring him. I'm not sure whether to referee or make popcorn and watch the show."

"Come for a ride with us and let's go eat," Bug suggested.

"Let me run to Pop's and see if your mom wants to take a ride. Maybe I can fix what's bothering her," I said as I stood up. I was proud of the fact that I could keep a straight face, but I almost lost it when Bug and Kitty raised their eyebrows and stared at me.

"Why are you two looking at him like that?" Sis asked Bug and Kitty before she looked at me. "What am I missing here?"

"I'm the one that sent her a gift, babe," I admitted. "She's worked up because of me."

"Why did you send her a gift?"

"Maybe we should go outside," Kitty suggested as he stood. Bug shot up from the recliner and started for the door, but I didn't give either of them a chance to leave before I explained things to Sis.

"I'm in love with your mom and have been for a long time, Sis. I finally started doing something about it, and she's not sure how to handle it. I guess cleaning is how she's dealing."

"You and my mom?"

Bug and Kitty were standing there like statues, only

their eyes moving as they watched our conversation like a tennis match.

"You okay with that?'

"It's about time, man. I thought you'd never put on your big girl panties and take charge," Sis yelled as she jumped up off the couch and threw herself into my arms. "What can I do to help?"

"Leave her be, don't say a word about it, just let me work my magic. If I need your help, I'll be in touch," I told her as I squeezed her tight. I let her go just far enough to look into her face, "You know how stubborn she can be. If any of us push too hard, she'll revolt just because she can."

"I'm so excited!" Sis hugged me one more time and then danced her way over to Bug. "Hook owes me $500!"

"What for?" Kitty asked the smiling girl.

"Almost a year ago, he bet me that Chef would never act on it, but I said he'd do it before next Christmas."

"You bet on me?"

"Of course! You're always a winner in my book."

"You guys hang out here for a few minutes, and let me go talk to Brea. I'll send Pop over, and maybe the three of you can talk him off the ledge."

"Not likely, but we'll listen to him rant for a while. Might make him feel better. You take your time," Bug said as he wiggled his eyebrows and held open the screen door for me.

"I'm playing the long game, Bug. I'll only be a minute or two."

"If that's all it takes, you should see a doctor. They've got pills for that now," Kitty called out from inside the house.

I put my hand up and flipped him off as I walked away. I could hear Sis and the other two laughing at me before I heard my screen door slam. I walked down the road until I got to Pop's, then let myself inside.

Sis was right. Pop was stomping around the house like a pissed off bull. I motioned for him to be quiet and then leaned down and whispered that he should go to my house for a while. He pursed his lips and did a full body shake, trying to calm himself down before he stomped out.

I walked across the living room toward the kitchen where I could hear Brea sifting through stuff and slamming things around while she grumbled under her breath. I could only make out a few words, but I knew she was cussing me.

"What are you so riled up about, Pickle?" I asked when I got right up behind her, blocking her in the pantry in front of me.

Brea let out a shout and whirled around. Her arm was up, ready to launch a can of corn at my head, so I reached up and grabbed her wrist. I used it to yank her toward me, and the can dropped to the ground when she slammed into my chest.

"You're not normally this high strung, sweetheart. What's got you all jittery?"

"Chef, we need to talk."

"What if I don't want to talk?"

"Well, you don't have a choice," Brea snapped as she tried to push out of my arms. "I'm not sure where this whole alpha-male bullshit came from, but you've got to tone it down a bit and let me talk."

"Alpha male?"

"The kind of man who thinks he needs to rescue the little woman from herself and won't even let her finish a sentence because he thinks he knows what's best for her. I need you to be more . . . a more understanding hero who listens to the woman's fears and respects them."

"Like in one of those books you're always reading?"

"Well, not exactly," Brea hedged.

"I'm like those men in your books, sugar."

"Is this the part where you tell me you're a shifter and turn into a werewolf on command, but you can't control your animal side?"

"A werewolf? What the fuck is a shifter? Are you drunk?"

"A werewolf! Duh."

"I'm a beast babe, but not a wolf."

Brea snorted. "Listen, Chef. First thing you're gonna have to do is give me my arm back. Then . . ."

"Seems I'm the one in charge here, Pickle," I murmured as I pulled her arms behind her back and grasped her wrists with one of my hands. That position pulled her shoulders back and put her body flush against mine. Brea leaned her head back and opened her mouth to start yelling, but I took that opportunity to sweep in and cover her mouth with mine.

Within seconds, she was kissing me back, and it was so hot, I was surprised we didn't ignite. I let my free hand roam up her body, brushing the outside of her breast as I moved it up to her neck. I wrapped my hand around the back of her neck as I leaned her back over my arm.

She started to fight me, afraid she might fall, but I pulled my mouth away from hers and whispered, "Trust me, baby. I've got you."

Brea started to shake her head, so I squeezed her neck just a bit and kissed her again. It took everything I had not to groan when her leg came up and wrapped around the back of my thigh. I was holding her up now, and she was too busy devouring my lips to even notice.

I kissed my way down her jaw and nipped at her earlobe with my teeth before I whispered, "Have you been thinking of our kiss in the barn, sugar? I can't sleep at night because every time I think of how you tasted, the little sounds you made in your throat when I kissed you, the way your body felt against mine, my cock gets so hard I have to take care of it. When you think of that first kiss, does it make you need to touch yourself?"

"It does," Brea whispered out in a sigh. "That's all I can think about. You're making me crazy, Marques."

"Tonight, when you're alone in bed, I want you to

think about this. Think about how good it feels when you let go for a minute and just feel." I ground my hard cock against her core and Brea moaned. "You feel how hard I get when I'm holding you, sugar?"

Brea moaned as her head fell back, and her eyes closed. I rubbed against her again, and she shivered.

"When you're in bed, I want you to think of me, Brea. I want you to call me when you're naked and wanting, and I'm gonna tell you everything I want to do to you and then listen to you come, baby. You gonna do that?"

"No. I can't do that. We can't . . ."

"Oh, we can definitely do that. And when we're on the phone and I hear you come, you're gonna be calling for me, Brea. You're gonna scream my name and clutch at the sheets, wishing it was me between your legs. And soon, when I get you naked underneath me, I'm gonna eat your pussy until you can't come anymore. I'm gonna lick you and suck on you until you're shaking and so hoarse you can't even talk. You know what I'm gonna do then?"

"What?" Brea shivered again, and I started to steadily rub my cock against her, knowing that she was so close, it would take just one nudge to get her off.

"I'm gonna slide into you, so slow you feel every inch. When you think that's all you can take, I'm going to push in even harder and fill you up. And when you're full of me . . ." I paused for a second and listened to Brea's pants get faster with the movement of my hips against her. "When you're full of me, I'm gonna pull out slowly and then slam my cock into you so hard, you see stars. I'm gonna do it over and over again until one more time, you're begging me to let you come. You wanna come, Brea? You want it?"

"I want it. Please, Marques. I want . . ."

I ground my cock against her and whispered in her ear, "Come now," right before I bit her on the neck.

Brea clenched her jaw and screamed through her teeth as she shook her head back and forth and clutched at me with her leg, holding me close to her, right where I needed to be.

I licked the spot I'd bitten and then sucked it into my mouth for a second so she'd see my mark on her later. Brea's breaths were slowing now, and I saw her eyes start to flutter as she came back to herself. I knew this was when I should make a hasty exit, but I had to taste her lips one more time.

I nipped my way up her jaw and then put my lips on hers in a soft, sweet kiss. Brea moaned and kissed me back as I slowly stood up. Her leg slid down over my hip, and her foot thumped when it hit the floor. When she was steady on her feet, I let her hands go. I reached up and put my other hand on her neck before I pulled back just a fraction to talk to her.

"Think about me tonight when you're in bed, sugar. Don't be shy if you need to call me so I can make you come again. It will be my pleasure. Believe me. And in the morning, I want you to drink your coffee out of that mug I sent you and remember that I like all the different parts of you. I like the soft parts, the pushy parts, that sassy mouth, and those prickly moods. I like them all, but I love *you*, Pickle. And soon you're gonna realize that it doesn't scare you nearly as much as you think it does. Soon, you'll realize it's okay to love me back."

I put one more soft kiss on Brea's lips and then turned and walked out of the pantry. I wasn't more than six feet away when I heard her whisper, "Oh, fuck me."

5

BREA

"What are we doing here again? And why do I have to pretend you're not with me?"

"Sky thinks there's something shady going on with one of Jack Bentley's sons. We were trying to find a way to keep an eye on him and found out he's going to be here schmoozing. The truck is the perfect place for one of us to hide and watch. Add to that, Boss wants to make sure that other food truck that always seems to have shady people in line is on the up and up."

"Okay, Hook. I'll bite. How in the hell are we going to know what this guy is doing just by watching him at this stupid thing, and did you bring your x-ray vision goggles to see through that trailer?"

"What the fuck is going on with you? You're awfully prickly lately."

"Are we here to analyze me or Bentley's kid?"

"See? That right there. You didn't deny it, you just snapped at me."

"I haven't been sleeping well."

"More dreams?"

"When I do sleep, yeah, I'm having the same old

nightmare. But the thing is, I'm really not sleeping all that much. I think that's what's doing it. And I've got a lot on my mind." I turned around and made myself a drink, adding an extra shot of espresso, hoping that would perk me up.

"What's on your mind?"

"I don't want to get into it with you, Hook."

"Why? I thought we were friends. Don't you talk about shit like that with friends?"

"You might be a little biased about this, so I'm not sure you're the right person to mull it over with. Hell, I don't have anyone I can talk to about this. I'll work it out," I lied before I blew on my coffee to cool it so I could take that first heavenly sip.

"If you can't talk to me, can you talk to the girls?"

"They pushed, I got snippy, and I'm avoiding them now."

"Then you'll just have to settle for talking to me. Now, let's talk about this thing."

I sighed, knowing the man wasn't going to drop it. How in the hell was I supposed to stay strong in my resolve when all I could do was think of Chef, and now, I needed to *talk* about him? I was going to explode.

I finally got a reprieve in the form of customers. They came along in a wave, and I was glad to have them. For the next half hour, there was a steady stream of students who had just finished classes at the college. They kept me on my toes, and by the time the line trickled down, I needed a quick break.

Just as I turned to pick up my now cold coffee for a sip, another customer walked up to the window. I recognized this man from the picture Boss and Hook had shown me. It was Jon Bentley, the man we were here to watch. He was joined in front of the trailer by another man, this one I recognized from television commercials he did to promote his car dealership.

The two men stood about six feet away from the trailer, staring at the menu while they talked in voices so low that kept me from hearing a word. I moved toward the coffee machine behind me and gave Hook the signal that our mark was just outside.

I turned back around and watched the two men for a second, reading their body language and studying them to figure out the best approach. Both successful businessmen in their own right, dressed for the country club, and completely ignoring the woman waiting in front of them. I was just about as important as a piece of furniture to them, serving a single purpose. I was almost positive that they'd assume I had the intelligence of a coffee table, so I decided to play toward that misconception. Finally, the two men got closer to the trailer, and I jumped into my spiel.

"Good afternoon! What can I get you handsome gentlemen today?" I used my bubbly, cheerful voice and schooled my face into the vacant look they most likely expected from one who was behind a food truck counter. I'd turned on the charm and turned up the Texas twang, just to add to the act.

"What does your Redhot Cider taste like?" the car dealer asked me.

"Um . . . I'm not sure how to explain it," I said before I let out a vapid giggle. "I can give you a sample, though!"

"Alright, sweetheart. That sounds fine," the man said condescendingly before he put one arm on the counter and leaned his body against it like he was ready to get comfortable and stay a while.

I glanced at the sugar dispenser Hook had put on the counter and was happy to see the listening device attached to the bottom of it was aimed right at the men. I couldn't hear what they were saying because of my movements inside the truck, but I knew the bug was one of Preacher's gadgets, and it could probably hear polar bears in Alaska from where it sat on the counter.

Once I had the sample cups ready, I pasted a smile on my face and turned back to the customers.

"Okay, good looking! Here's your sample. I didn't know if you'd want one, sir, so I took the liberty of making one for you too. I've also got our Mexican hot chocolate here for you to try."

"Thanks, sweetheart," Jon, the realtor, said dismissively as he picked up one of the small cups and took a sip.

While the two men talked and sipped on the samples I'd given them, I busied myself rearranging things that were just fine where they were and wiping off counter space that was already pristine. Finally, one of the men rapped his knuckles on the counter and called, "Hey, darlin'!"

I giggled again, and a pain shot from my right eyeball through my brain all the way down my spine. This was bullshit.

"We'll each take one of those hot chocolates, and I'd like a pecan brownie," the car salesman told me as he stared at my chest.

I took that opportunity to lean forward and rest my arms on the counter, pushing my boobs together for just the right amount of cleavage while I smiled at them.

"We're having a drawing for the business owners who leave me their cards. We'll have three lucky winners. If you win, you'll get a gift basket delivered to your office next week. Would either of you be interested?"

"Oh, I'm interested," the slimy car salesman said to my boobs as he reached for his wallet. The realtor pulled a business card out of the pocket on the front of his dress shirt and handed it over. The car salesman held his card out, and when I tried to take it, he wouldn't let go. He smiled when he asked, "Will you deliver the prize yourself?"

"I sure will, sweetheart," I assured him before I winked and grinned.

I took the cards and dropped them into a fishbowl we'd set aside for just this opportunity before I filled their order. I handed the men their drinks, gave the car salesman his brownie, and pushed a few buttons on the iPad to get their total.

"You keep the change, sweetheart. I look forward to seeing you in my office when I win."

"You seem pretty sure you'll get lucky," I told him as I reached out and touched his forearm.

"I'm the kind of man that always gets what he wants, darlin'. Always."

I giggled again and squeezed his arm before I drew my hand back.

I watched the two men amble away. When they were a good distance from the trailer, I let out a heavy sigh.

"That hurt, didn't it?" Hook asked with a laugh.

"Can you see my eye twitching?" I asked Hook when I turned to look at him. "I think I'm about to have an aneurysm or something."

Hook laughed again. "You were awfully convincing. You're pretty good at reading people, B. You did good."

"Okay, well, we got that set-up accomplished. I don't know what the microphone picked up, but maybe there's something there. Now what?"

"Now we finish our conversation," Hook urged.

"It's nothing."

"Nothing? I think it's crazy that you'd refer to anything regarding Chef as little, but that's just me. The man's as big as a doorway, Brea, I'm sure you noticed."

"How do you know that it's Chef I'm thinking about?"

"B, don't bullshit a bullshitter. You've had it bad for him for a while now. I noticed it when he came home to Tenillo last year for a visit. You saw the man in a whole new light, and it knocked you on your ass."

"I saw him in a whole new light again a few weeks ago, Hook, and any dream I'd had of us together vanished."

"Why? Because he got shot? You're not going to ditch my ass because I got shot, are you?"

"Oh, I'm plenty pissed about that. I'm even pissed that someone shot Preacher even though I've been dreaming of doing that for years now." I tried to change the subject but knew by the look on Hook's face that it wasn't happening, so I just powered on. There was no sense beating around the bush. "You remember when Ray died, Hook. It damn near broke me. Sis too."

"Yeah. But you got through it, and so did she. What does that have to do with Chef? Are you feeling guilty because of Ray, sweetheart?"

"No, not at all. He'd be pissed if he thought I was going to brood about him forever. All he ever wanted was for me to be happy."

"Okay, well, that's one hurdle I'm glad we don't have to jump. Now what's that got to do with Chef?"

"He got shot, Hook. Not because he was in the wrong place at the wrong time but because he put himself in danger knowing the risk he was taking. I sat there with bandages trying to make sure he didn't bleed all over the place, and he acted like it was no big deal at all."

"It just didn't affect him. I literally still have a pain in my ass, but Chef's just right as rain, like nothing happened. The man's a beast."

"Stop whining. You're fine. Good grief."

"God. I get no fucking respect from you people," Hook complained. "Let me get this straight, B. You're going to ignore the man who's been head over heels for you for years because you're afraid he's gonna die. That's a special kind of stupid. Newsflash! We're all gonna die someday."

"We will, but I already buried the man I love. I know for a fact I won't survive having to do that shit again, Hook. I just can't . . . I won't take that chance. I've got to consider Sis too. Her feelings run deeper than people might think. If I let him into our lives and we lose him, it will be all my fault when her heart is broken."

"Sis and I have known forever that Chef's in love with you. She's not one to pick up on subtleties like that, but years ago, before Ray even passed, she noticed that Chef got this dreamy expression on his face when he looked at you."

"Bullshit."

"He moved because he couldn't bear to stay in Tenillo and watch you from a distance, and he felt bad because he'd become friends with Ray. He knew he'd never be able to find someone and settle down if he was here pining for you, B. He's loved you for that long."

"No, he has not," I scoffed. "The other night at Jenn's house, he found me crying in the barn. He got a wild hair up his ass that he could comfort me, and next thing you know, he's got me in his arms, kissing me senseless. Then, he's mauling me in Pop's pantry, telling me he loves me and making me fucking think about him all the time. I can't get a good night's sleep for shit between my nightmares about what happened that night and thinking of Chef. I haven't slept more than an hour or two at a time in weeks.

Something's gotta give."

"What are you going to do about it?"

"I'm going to go on the way I have before. I'll keep myself busy, take care of things, and keep them just the way I like them. I've got no room in my life for a man who's gonna put himself in danger all the time and leave me here alone. Ray couldn't help what happened. Chef can but won't. Therefore, I've set my mind to it. I'm going to avoid him at all costs, ignoring the fucking sweet presents he keeps sending me. I'm just going to focus on what I've got going."

"You've got control issues."

"I just like for things to be a certain way, Hook."

"You like to be in charge. Chef is not the kind of guy to let that happen. I think that's part of the problem. He's not the kind of man you can run over and push around."

"Ray wasn't the kind . . ."

"Honey, Ray wasn't either. That's why you loved him. For once in your life, you found someone you could hand the reins off to and trust to help keep things moving. You lost him, and now, you're so rigid about shit that you just can't see the forest for the trees."

I turned when I heard a customer at the window, happy for a reprieve from this conversation. Hook was going to have to move the fuck on to a different topic. He was hitting way too close to home for me right now. The last thing I needed was to curl up on the floor and gut myself crying.

No. I had less than an hour left here at the park, then

maybe an hour at Jenn's house to drop off the trailer and get everything settled. After that, I was going to go home and lose myself in a new LLV release that had dropped on my Kindle this morning and forget the world around me.

I was not going to think about what Hook had said, and I was damn sure not going to think of Chef while I sipped my coffee out of my new favorite mug or snuggled up under the soft blanket he'd had delivered to me today.

I wasn't going to think of him tonight while I was alone in bed, and I sure as hell wasn't going to call him and let him talk dirty to me until I had another mind-blowing orgasm.

I could be strong. I would be strong. I didn't have any other choice.

"I'll get Phantom to send Preacher a copy of this recording, and we'll let them see if they can hear what the two were talking about."

"You said the guy from the picture was talking to that car salesman from the television commercials?" Jenn asked from her stool at the bar.

"Yeah. You know that guy with the annoying fucking jingle that sticks in your head? That guy. What's his name?" I leaned my head back and looked at the ceiling as I played that annoying radio commercial and heard his voice squawking about car deals in my head.

"Fairchild Motors. His name is Cyrus."

"That's it!" I smiled over at Executioner, one of the men from the Ares Infidels, and then shook my head. "That jingle on his radio ad is enough to make me stab my own ears with an ice pick."

Executioner laughed before he agreed, "Isn't it, though?"

"She flirted with those guys like she was born to do it. It was so weird hearing her giggle like some airhead," Hook told the men. "She flipped a switch and went from the Brea we know to some woman I wouldn't recognize on the street. She had Fairchild eating that shit up. He couldn't take his eyes off her chest."

"What a pig," Jenn grumbled. "I've seen those men together before. More than once, actually. They come to the truck and get their coffee before they walk around wherever we're at for a while and then they split up and go their own way. I've noticed them because that car guy is always so condescending. It's like he expected me to be some giggling, stupid set of tits who's just there to hang on his every word."

"Brea giggled, Jenn. More than once," Hook told her seriously. He put his hand up on his chest and tried to sound like me. He giggled and then reached out and touched Jenn's arm before he giggled again.

I couldn't help but laugh when I saw Executioner, Sin, and Boss grimace like they'd just smelled something bad.

"Brea's not the giggling type. At all." Jenn laughed softly as she shook her head. "That had to hurt."

"I think I pulled something."

The men laughed at my disgust, and soon, I was laughing with them as Hook kept up his act, chasing Sin around the dining room table and trying to touch him while he yelled in a high-pitched voice, "Come here, big boy! Give Hook some sugar!"

Sin suddenly realized he was running from someone and stopped dead in his tracks, spun around, and pointed his finger in Hook's face. He growled, "I will fuck you up!"

Hook didn't even flinch. He wiggled his eyebrows and whispered, "Bring it, stud."

"Oh shit!" Executioner slapped the counter and leaned forward as he held his stomach and laughed. He had tears running down his cheeks as we watched Sin try to keep a straight face while Hook shimmied his hips in front of him.

"Oh God." Jenn gasped as she messed with her phone. I heard my phone ding at the same time as everyone else's. When I looked down, I saw that Jenn had videoed the whole thing and sent it to us.

"You did not just . . ." Sin growled as he pulled his phone out of his pocket. He put it up to his ear and sighed. "Hey, sweetheart," he answered. He held the phone away from his ear and looked at it before he growled at Hook and pushed the button to end the call. "That was Lyric. She told me to invite you and Paula over for dinner next week. She said she'd get with Paula and find out your favorite dessert because she owes you for giving her such a laugh."

We were all laughing now, and Sin just shook his head.

"Oh God." Executioner reached up to wipe the tears

off his face. "That was fucking awesome. Jenn, do you have everyone's number, or do I need to . . ."

"Oh, I've got *everyone's* number," Jenn assured him and never looked up from her phone. I laughed when her phone started vibrating uncontrollably as people responded to her text. She snickered as she scrolled through her messages and then looked up at Sin. "Your mom says hello."

"No fucking respect. None."

"I feel ya, Sin. Absolutely nada." Boss commiserated as he looked down at the floor with a dramatic sigh.

"I'm going home, Jenn," I told my friend as the guys started bitching about the women in their lives and all the things they did that irritated them. "I've got everything cleaned up already."

"Are we okay, Brea? I'm sorry about the other day. . ."

"No. I'm sorry I was so short with you girls. I overreacted because what we were talking about hit too close to home."

"Is everything alright now?"

"The man is making me fucking crazy," I admitted.

"They do that. On purpose, I'm sure."

"I'm going to go home, read a book, and get lost for a while. I'll give you a call in a few days so we can make those damn gift baskets the guys need us to do."

"Okay. Call if you need me, okay?"

"I will."

"Promise?'

"I promise. I'm gonna sneak out while they're distracted. I'll talk to you guys later."

Jenn nodded and turned around to watch the guys who were standing around the dining room table. I slipped out the back door and walked across the sunroom to go to my car.

The weather was gorgeous, and I wondered if Chef was out on his motorcycle, enjoying the sunshine.

I wondered if he was thinking about me because I couldn't get the man out of my head.

6

BREA

"We just walk into the man's office, offer him the gift basket, and leave?"

"Actually, I need you to take it one step further. Both guys are all into tech and gadgets from what Preacher can find on them. I need you to make sure you give the mug straight to the guy," Phantom told me. "I want you to show him how cool it is and all the things this plain-looking insulated mug can do. It makes sense since you were working at a coffee truck when they met you."

"The coffee mug does tricks?" I asked with one eyebrow raised.

"Ah, yes, it does," Phantom said with a wicked laugh. "It's got a battery pack that keeps the drink warm without warming up the exterior."

"Shit. Why are we giving it away then?" Frankie asked as she picked the mug up and studied the base.

"Even better, it's got this port on the bottom that lets you recharge it. It even works as a spare charger for your phone. All you've got to do is plug the USB into your computer or a wall charger. Takes about four hours to get a full charge."

"I want one," I told Phantom when I took the mug out of his hands. "That's handy. Keeps your coffee warm, charges your phone . . ."

"If it could just give me an orgasm and cuddle me at night, it would be the total package," Frankie joked.

"No shit," I agreed. "Maybe cook occasionally too."

"If these guys are crooked, why are we giving them cool gadgets and a gift basket full of goodies?"

"Yeah. That's what I want to know."

Phantom was smiling when he reached out and took the mugs out of our hands.

"Make sure to explain that they have to hand wash the mugs. They can't go into the dishwasher, or they won't work anymore."

"Okay. That makes sense, I guess. The battery pack would die from the heat, right?"

"Well, Brea, not only would the battery pack be shot, but so would the chip inside that's going to install a hidden app on their phones that allows us to see everything they text and all of their contacts. It will also infect their computer with a virus, and give us an in through their firewall and virus software."

"No shit," Frankie whispered. She looked up at Phantom with eyes as wide as mine. "You can do that?"

"Honey, we can do all sorts of things if given time and opportunity," Phantom drawled.

"That kind of makes me want to go live in a cave with no electronics," I admitted. "That's some intrusive shit, and he'll never even know. What if neither of them are doing anything shady?"

"Then we won't find anything we need," Phantom said with a shrug. "Now, remember, you have to tell him he can never put the mug in the dishwasher."

"Got it," Frankie assured him.

"Santa is going to be your escort today. He's going to go inside and look around while the two of you flash some cleavage and distract the men. You cool with all that?"

I snorted and shrugged one shoulder.

"You know you're dying to hang out with me, Brea. Admit it!" Santa called out from the couch in the living room where he was sprawled.

Phantom smiled and continued, "The backstory is that Brea works for Jenn, and Frankie is going to buy into her business. You might need another vehicle someday while you're at the dealership, and you might be thinking of opening a cafe while you're at the realtor's office. Frankie, make sure and let Bentley and Fairchild know that you're a doctor at the hospital so they see dollar signs and upper crust country club shit. Brea, Fairchild took a shine to you, so you'll schmooze him, okay? Frankie, Brea didn't seem like Bentley's type, so he's yours."

"Why do I get the smarmy car salesman while she gets the cute realtor? That shit's just not fair."

"If these men are involved in what we suspect, smarmy car salesman is the least of his flaws," Phantom said in a low voice. "Anyway, schmooze the man you're assigned to, and see if you can get him to show you around the office. Make sure that Santa is right there with you if you get a tour, okay?"

"We need a bodyguard?" Frankie asked, wondering just what she'd gotten into when Boss asked her to volunteer for this delivery gig.

"No, not as far as I know. If it came down to it, Santa would protect you with his life, but that's not why we want him to go with you. Who better to assess the weakness and strengths of a building than a man who spent the majority of his younger years robbing people blind?" Boss asked.

"No shit." I chuckled. "We're the distraction, and Santa's there to case the joint."

"Exactly," Phantom agreed.

"It's so weird that I'm sitting here with a cop planning nefarious shit. Where were you when I was rustling livestock, big guy?"

"I believe I was serving time for a murder conviction," Boss drawled.

"You were a rustler? That shit still happens?" Phantom asked. "I thought that was from back in the wild west days."

"Technically, it still happens. That's what I was convicted of the first time. I sold a prized bull and some horses that didn't belong to me and used the money to buy drugs."

"Our sweet little shit kicker," Boss teased.

"You were in prison?" Frankie balked. I could hear the shock in her voice, and I had to laugh.

"Twice," I admitted. "I'm hard-headed and didn't learn my lesson the first time."

"You stole another cow?"

"That's not why I went in the second time, but it was a bull, honey, not a cow."

"I didn't realize there was a difference," Frankie said with a shrug.

I heard Boss snort, and then he and Phantom started chuckling.

"A bull has his balls, Frankie; a steer doesn't. A cow is a female that's there for either giving birth to more cows, beef, or milk."

"Oooh." Frankie slowly nodded her head.

"You are such a big city girl," Boss said as he patted our new friend on the shoulder. "Not even the slightest bit country, but hey, you're learning, right?"

"I guess. Can we get this show on the road? I've got a spa appointment at four."

"Big city girl, for sure. We can't get in the way of that, can we?" Phantom said sarcastically. "If we can get Santa off his ass, we'll get you two on the road."

"Thanks for doing this, ladies. We appreciate it."

"No problem, Boss," Frankie told him with a smile as

she hopped down off her stool.

I smiled at my friend and tilted my head in his direction. "Of course, Boss. Whatever you need, I'm your girl."

"Always, Brea."

"How do I look?" I asked Santa as he helped me out of Jenn's truck.

Santa had already moved back a few steps and was opening the door for Frankie when he said, "You look funny. I don't like it."

"I look funny?"

"She does not!" Frankie pushed Santa's shoulder when she snapped at him. "Be nice."

"Yes, ma'am," Santa murmured. "I don't mean funny like ha-ha, Brea. I mean you don't look like you. You're prettier when you're wearing your t-shirt and jeans. You look too high maintenance dressed up like that. I've never seen you all dolled up before."

"I know there's a compliment in there somewhere if I just dig around deep enough," I teased Santa. I could tell that Frankie was irritated with him, and from the look on her face, she did not appreciate his 'high maintenance' comment at all. Hoping to stop an argument before it progressed, I motioned Santa toward the truck and said, "Carry our shit, minion."

"That's more like it, right there. I see Brea now."

Santa reached into the truck and pulled out the large square basket we'd arranged before we left Jenn's. I made sure nothing had been displaced on the drive and then looked over at Santa. He was looking at Frankie, who was still frowning.

"What's wrong, Big City?" Santa asked.

"Just because a woman likes to look pretty doesn't mean she's high maintenance. And my name is Francesca, thank you very much."

"Francesca," Santa said the word like he was trying to get a taste of it, slowly drawing all the syllables out as he stared at Frankie. He snapped out of it and asked, "Are you all gussied up because you want to be or because you think that's what other people want to see?"

"What business is that of yours?" Frankie snapped.

"Children! Let's focus on the task at hand, okay?"

Santa shot me a wicked grin. I knew he was just messing with Frankie, and from the gleam in his eye, it wasn't difficult to see why.

"Brea, did you let Chef know what we were doing this morning?"

"Why would I tell Chef?"

Santa raised one eyebrow in question but didn't answer me.

"What he's saying, using his facial expressions because all the big words hurt his brain, is that he thinks you need to get permission from Chef to do things. Now, Brea,

Santa's . . . hold on. I just can't with that name. What is your *real* name?"

"Christopher," Santa answered with a grin.

"Christopher? Really? Anyway, Brea, *Christopher* is a neanderthal, so make sure you speak slowly and use plenty of hand gestures. That's how they talked back in the Stone Age."

I pulled my lips in between my teeth and took a deep breath through my nose. I was almost successful in choking back my laughter.

Santa started grunting and pointing toward the building ahead of us. Frankie actually growled at him, and that was the last straw. I lost it and my laughter rang out and echoed off the buildings around us.

"I just had the funniest thought," I told my friends. Both of them looked at me, and I continued, "We're a literal joke."

"What?"

"Two ex-cons and a doctor walk into a car dealership . . ."

CHEF

"What did you have delivered to her today?"

I looked at Hook and then eyed Hannigan, the cop we were watching, before I answered. "Silk scarves. They should get there sometime this afternoon. How did you know I was having stuff delivered?"

"Cap mentioned it when we were at Boss's planning the follow-up thing that the girls are doing today."

"The thing? What thing?"

"Why silk scarves?"

"What. Thing."

"They're delivering prize baskets to the winners of Jenn's drawing," Hook answered, looking at me curiously.

"The girls? Which girls? Brea went, but did Paula go with her?"

"Why does it have to be my woman?"

"Your woman has an arsenal in her bra, man. She's a good bet."

"Nah. It was Brea and Frankie. Santa's with them to look around the buildings, if he can."

"Frankie. I don't know much about her. Seems nice."

"She's Paula's best friend. She's probably got a flamethrower in her boot or something."

"They're just dropping the gifts off?"

"No, the plan is to meet with those guys and get them talking. The girls got all dressed up to flirt and shit."

"What?" I spat as I let the bar clank down onto the frame.

"Chill. All eyes are on us right now, brother," Hook whispered. I didn't look around, but I realized that the gym was quieter than usual. I reached up and started another round of lifts. Hook's face was upside down, and it was almost hard to take him seriously when he started talking again. "Brea's doing this one thing for us, man. She can take care of herself better than most, even without an arsenal in her bra. Have you seen the deadly accurate aim she has? She can knock you in the head with whatever's handy from across the room."

"Not thrilled with her putting herself out there more than she already has, Hook."

"Well, she's a big girl and can make her own decisions. Besides, she's with Santa. You know he's got her back."

I had done too many reps and was having difficulty getting the bar back in place. I couldn't comment on what Hook had said, I could only grunt with the effort I was expending. Hook realized I was struggling and helped me lift the bar onto the frame.

Finished with our upper body work, Hook and I moved over to the leg press machine. Once I had my weights set, I sat down to begin my reps, my mind out there somewhere with Brea. I wasn't pissed that she was set to flirt with some nameless asshole, I was upset that she could be putting herself in the line of fire with all the shit going on in this town.

Not that she wasn't already in the middle of it, considering the company she kept everyday, but I didn't want her associated with what we were trying to do. I wanted her to stay on the perimeter where it was safer. If something was discovered and that put her in the crosshairs, she could be in danger.

I couldn't stand that thought. Brea and Sis had been through enough. They didn't know it yet, but it was my job to see that the rest of their lives were smooth sailing. Sis probably wouldn't have a problem with it. As a matter of fact, her reaction the other night seemed like a ringing endorsement. Brea, on the other hand, was going to resist me at every turn.

"You never did say why you sent Brea silk scarves" Hook said between sets. "Brea doesn't seem the type to wear that sort of shit, man. Pretty sure that gift will be a dud."

I turned and stared at my friend as my lips curled up into a smile. "Not for her to wear, bud."

"Aw, man," Hook whined when he got what I was saying. "I don't wanna know that shit. She's like a sister to me."

"Well, if that's the case, I've got something going on with your niece you might want to know about."

"Sis? What's going on?"

"When I first met her, I made a deal that if she won a bet, I'd help her convince you and Boss to build her a bike."

"She's been after us about that for years."

"Well, it's off your plate. I'm picking her up for lunch today, and we're going to Executioner's shop to look at bikes."

"I thought she wanted to build her own."

"She does. We're going to get a read on what size frame she needs. She's a little thing, so I want to make sure we get the right base."

"You might talk to her. Last thing I heard, she was very specific about what she wanted. You know Sis - there's no changing her mind about shit."

"Oh, she knows what she wants. A purple 1993 Softail. I just want to make sure that's something she can ride before we go hunting down parts and pieces. There goes Hannigan," I said in a soft voice as I watched the woman walk out of the gym, again with a bag she hadn't walked in with.

"I've got an idea."

"What?"

"We buy some ski masks and mug that bitch when she leaves here. I'm that curious about what exactly she's carting around."

"Pretty sure mugging is not part of the master plan, man."

Hook sighed.

"I know that the urge to just say fuck it and smash shit is overwhelming, Hook, but we gotta look at the long game. What's she doing up here all the time and what is she carrying out? Better yet, where's she taking whatever's in the bag? We'll figure it out. Patience, my man. Patience."

"How's that working out for you with Brea?"

"Baby steps, brother."

7

BREA

"You want another glass of wine, Jenn?" I called out as I walked over to refill my own glass.

"Please!" I heard Jenn call down from her bedroom. I peeked up at the balcony where I could see into her room, but she wasn't there. "I'm dealing with animal issues right now. Moe and Elvira are pissed and won't come out of the shower."

"How many animals does this woman have?" Blue, one of my good friends, had a rare night off and had agreed to join us for girl's night at Jenn's.

The guys were all together out in the man cave they'd created in the old well house, and Jenn wanted us to hang out for a while.

"Umpteen. All kinds. You haven't even seen the fun ones yet. I guess they're still upstairs with her," Paula answered.

"If you think Jenn's animals are crazy, wait til you visit Paula's. She's a cat lady like no other," Frankie teased.

"Yeah, Jenn's got a soft heart for animals. Hook plays up to that and asks her to 'help' him with whatever rescue he takes in. They both say it's just until he finds a good home, but we all know she's never letting any of them go anywhere."

"I saw that cat over there. It's the size of a dog," Blue said as she nodded toward one of Boss's cats stretched out on the back of the couch.

"Yeah, Paula's cat has that one beat. Jenn, on the other hand, has quite the variety of pets."

As if I'd called them, I heard Jenn's menagerie start down the stairs.

"Is that a fucking skunk?" Blue yelled as she crawled up onto the bar. "Holy shit! And what's that?"

"Oh, those are alpacas!" Jenn said cheerfully as she got to the bottom of the stairs.

"No!" Blue yelled as she pointed at an animal I didn't recognize.

"Oh, that's BB. She's a Rottweiler," Jenn explained as she walked closer to us. She trailed her hand up the newest dog's back before she perched on one of the barstools and pulled her wine glass closer to her. "She's gonna stay with us until Hook finds her a forever home."

"What's wrong with her?" Paula asked as she stared down at the dog.

"She's . . . well . . . she's plus size."

I was taking a sip of my wine when I heard that explanation and nearly spit it everywhere. Once I was able to swallow and get my coughing under control, I asked, "Plus size? What does that mean? Do you buy her collars at Lane Bryant?"

Paula and Frankie started cackling, and Jenn just

shook her head.

"I can't say anything. I've got a few extra pounds on me," Blue admitted as she eyed all the animals warily from her perch on the bar. "I just don't know which scares me more - the skunk giving me a go to hell look from the couch, the dog that looks like it ate a beach ball, or . . . that *is* a rooster, right?"

"That's Ed Earl."

"Do you live under power lines?" Blue asked as she glanced out the front window. "Why are half your animals plus size?"

"Why *are* my animals so freaking big?" Jenn asked as she glanced around at all of them. "I never even considered that."

"At Brea's house, everything is miniature," Blue pointed out. "I come over here, and it's like an alternate universe. Next thing you're gonna tell me is there's a circus out back with lions, tigers, and bears."

"Oh my!" Frankie added.

"No. That's my house!" Paula started laughing as she watched Blue get down off the bar.

"None of them are going to eat me, are they?" Blue asked. She took a good look at David and Sammy, Jenn's alpacas and then she was lost. "Oh my goodness, they're just the cutest!"

"And there she goes," I mused as I watched my friend drop to her knees to love on the animals.

"Did I tell you that they let me bring them up to Pop's rehab place before they released him? The residents just ate Sammy and David up."

"I can see that happening," Paula told her as she reached down to rub Sammy's head.

"At least Hook doesn't give me animals left and right. I made sure he understood that Bruce was the last one. No more. I've got plenty of mouths to feed, and I'm not taking any more of his strays." Paula looked over at me with wide eyes, and I tilted my head and stared at her. "What am I missing here, Paula?"

"Nothing, Brea. Nothing at all," Paula lied. "Moving right along. How are things going with your gifts? What else have you gotten since the last time we talked?"

Blue looked up, curious now, "Gifts?"

"Chef's been sending her gifts every other day or so for a few weeks now. He has them delivered to wherever she is," Jenn explained.

"First, she got a coffee mug and then a snuggly blanket. Last Friday, she got a box of beautiful silk scarves. I'm not sure what's up with those," Frankie said as she looked at me. "Brea doesn't seem like the scarf-wearing type."

"She got a certificate for a spa day on Monday. Did you go to the appointment?"

"I did," I admitted begrudgingly. I'd sworn it was going to go to waste, that I didn't have time to go and get pampered, but I'd caved. The thought of a massage and a day of relaxation won me over, and I kept the appointment on

Tuesday.

"Did you do *all* of the scheduled treatments?" Frankie asked with a grin.

"I did. I'll admit that I was skeptical, but the waxing didn't hurt nearly as bad as I thought it would."

"Hmm. What were the other gifts?" Paula asked as she propped her chin in her hands. Blue took her seat, and all eyes were on me. I took a sip of my wine and sighed.

"Wednesday's gift was a satin blindfold and a box of candles. Today's gift was different. He gave me an assortment of pickles. There's like a dozen jars of different kinds of pickles waiting for me at home right now. You're lucky I'm even here."

"Hmm."

"What's the fucking 'hmm' for, Paula? What do you know?"

"He's plotting your seduction," Blue told us. "You can't see it?"

"I see it," Jenn told her as she smiled widely and nodded.

"Oh, I see it too."

"What the fuck are y'all talking about?"

"What did the cards say?" Jenn asked me.

"I don't remember."

"Where are they?" Blue asked with a grin. Without

even thinking, I glanced at my purse. I was just about to open my mouth to lie and say I'd thrown them away when Blue jumped up and grabbed my bag. She found the stack of small envelopes instantly and pulled them out before I could even argue. "Okay, the first one was the coffee mug, right? *'Don't get all prickly. Enjoy your coffee and think of me.'* Then we've got the blanket. *'Wrap this around you when I'm not there.'*"

"That's sweet," Jenn said as she looked over Blue's shoulder and read the next one. "Oh! *'I'm sure your beautiful skin is even softer. I can't wait to compare.'* That's promising."

"He's so tying you up with those scarves."

"Like hell," I growled.

"The next one was with the spa certificate, right?" Frankie asked as she leaned close to Blue. *"'Relax and enjoy. I don't want anything to get in the way of your comfort or your pleasure.'* Oh, he's thinking about getting his mouth on all your girly bits, Brea."

I leaned my head back and stared at the ceiling while I wondered why I'd never called and gotten prices on backhoe rentals. Blue read the next card.

"'All five of your senses are important, my love.' Oh, my goodness. He's got the silk scarves and the blanket for touch, the blindfold for sight, the candles for smell, and the coffee mug and the pickles for taste. She loves pickles."

I sighed, realizing that the girls were right. I hadn't put all that together until just now. The man was seducing me from afar.

"He missed hearing," Paula pointed out.

CEE BOWERMAN

"Have you heard that man's voice?" Jenn had a full body shiver.

Frankie tilted her glass toward Jenn and nodded. "Point made there, sister. Good Lord, it's so deep and growly. He should narrate audiobooks."

"He could read me the back of a shampoo bottle, and I'd be able to work up an orgasm or two," Blue told the girls. "Can you imagine phone sex with that man?"

"Can you imagine him whispering next to your ear while he nibbles on your neck?" Frankie asked before she shivered. "Thank you for my orgasm, sir. May I have another?"

"Mmhhmm," Paula hummed. "Has anyone else noticed the man's hands?"

"Why in the hell are we talking about this? Why? Just why? Jesus, y'all are as horny as a bunch of women who've been locked up for a fucking year."

"Eh, they're not that bad," Blue pointed out. "By the time you've been in there a year, you kind of become immune."

"You've been to prison too?" Frankie nearly squeaked. "Holy shit. Did you rustle cattle with Brea?"

I stopped staring at the ceiling and let my head fall forward until my chin was resting on my chest.

"No. The closest I've ever been to a cow is when I chew up a bite of steak."

"So, what did you do?" Frankie asked softly, and I

saw Blue smile.

"Bad etiquette, Frankie!" Paula snapped.

"Oh! Shit! Sorry."

"It's not a secret. A quick internet search would tell you. I was already on probation for a few things, but I got into an altercation with a woman and went to prison for it."

"You went to prison for fighting?"

"Eh, it started out that way, but she ended up dead. That wasn't my intention when we started, but some people just need killing, you know?"

"Preach it, sister," Jenn agreed as she held her glass up. Blue and the rest of us clinked our wine glasses against hers and took a long drink. At the same time, we heard motorcycles out front and turned to look out the window. There was a line of motorcycles followed by a truck pulling into the driveway. "Looks like Lyric and the rest of them are here. Brea, will you help me get the herd out to the back porch?"

"Do we need a dolly for the new dog, or can she waddle her way outside?"

"Be nice, she's sensitive!" Jenn scolded. "You'll hurt her feelings."

"I'd hope it might hurt her appetite," Paula grumbled as she picked Elvira up off the back of the couch.

I grabbed the canister where Jenn kept her homemade pet treats and shook the string of bells she had attached to it. All of the animals, including Boss's cat, perked up and followed me out to the back porch.

As I doled out treats and got the animals settled with Paula, I heard Jenn and Frankie start talking about the notes we'd left laying on the bar. By the time I stood up to go back inside, Lyric, Jackie, and Skye were speculating about Chef's next move right along with the rest of the girls.

I saw Paula grinning from ear to ear.

It hit me. An excavator was for bigger projects. With the body count I was facing, I'd need something more than just a backhoe.

CHEF

"I talked to Jenn about it a little bit more, and we even got Paula in on the conversation. Apparently, when there's some sort of gathering, Bentley and Fairchild show up, walk around, and chat for a while. Now, that begs the question, what the fuck do those two have to talk about?"

"Maybe they're just friends," Santa said with a shrug. "Shit. Maybe they're secret lovers or something. No telling."

"Fairchild is the one that rented Julia's apartment for her," Boss pointed out.

"Still, maybe he likes to dip his toes in all sorts of water."

"Sexual preferences aside, there's something shady about the car guy, and Skye's convinced there's something shady going on at the realtor's office. The fact that they keep hooking up to chat is odd in and of itself, but you add those little nuggets in there, and it seems that there's something bigger at play," Sin pointed out. "We left the girls at the house when we came back here, but I can call Skye if you guys want to hear her intel on the realtor's office."

"Nah, man. I got ya," Santa told Sin. "Women have an intuition about shit anyway, you know?"

"They seem to," Executioner agreed. "They sure seem to."

"Your prospect is some voodoo priest or something," I told the men. "Creeped me the hell out the way he looked into that asshole's eyes. Like he was looking all the way down into his black soul or some shit."

I couldn't help but shiver, and I saw Santa do the same. When I glanced at Boss, he was smiling.

"He has a certain talent, doesn't he?" Sin asked sarcastically before he and Executioner laughed.

"Hook had a suggestion while we were at the gym. I know there are a lot of moving parts here, but the more I think about what he came up with, the more I think it just might work."

"I said that we should buy some ski masks and just mug the cop lady. We'll take the bag she carries off her hands and find out what she's got. We can string her up and have the prospect look deep into her eyes and get her to spill what she knows," Hook told our group.

"Leave it to the convict to come up with a plan that includes kidnapping a law enforcement officer," Bug teased.

"I think Hannigan is a small fry in the grand scheme of things. I say we take Hook's idea and just do that to Bentley and this Fairchild guy. String 'em up out at Sin's place, work 'em over, and get Omen to work his voodoo magic," Santa suggested. "I know with circumstances and all, it might be necessary, but I'm not sure I'm game for torturing a woman."

I saw a few of the men around the table nod in agreement.

"Shit. If we ever come across a situation where we need to deal with a woman like that, we just pull Paula out of our pocket. I mean that literally. Have you noticed how short she is?" Pitbull laughed along with the rest of us, knowing Paula would probably punch him in the dick if she heard him talking about her like that.

"Paula *and* Frankie," Hook said after everyone calmed down. "Frankie and Paula are tight and have been for years. I think there's some untapped resources inside that woman, and it almost scares me to imagine opening them up."

I happened to be looking at Santa when Hook mentioned Frankie and didn't miss the grin that spread across his face. When he looked at me, I just shook my head. That one was almost as prickly as my Brea. He had his work cut out for him.

"Have you met our friend Blue? She just moved back to town. She'd be another one in our arsenal. All we'd have to say is that whoever we had tied up in the barn hurt an animal or a kid, and she'd be all over them," Captain told the guys. "She's at the house right now getting to know the other girls."

"Jesus. That's terrifying," Preacher mumbled. "That's all we fucking need. Put them all together and unsupervised, and there's no telling what sort of shit they'll get into. Sin, Ex, you two need to go gather up your women and take them home. Blue's scary as all hell and mean as a damn snake."

"You think Brea's mean, too, Preach. Are you just scared of women in general?" I asked my old friend with a laugh.

"They're not normal women, Chef. None of them. Not one of those damn females has a soft side, I don't care what you boys say."

"Now, don't be insulting our women, Preacher," Boss warned.

"I'm not saying that to be ugly, I'm just pointing out facts. Maybe Sin and Ex's old ladies do. I bet that sweet Jackie does too. But you rile them up, and they can summon their crazy, I'm sure. On a regular day, Jenn's bossy as all hell, Paula's a razor blade-carrying psycho, Brea's got a mouth on her that could make a deaf person cringe, and Frankie's a wild card. Now you're saying Blue is home, and that's just icing on the crazy cake. Makes my stomach hurt just imagining them together and plotting shit." Preacher grimaced. "I need some Tums."

"I hate to admit it, but he's right about Lyric. When she's riled, she's a pistol," Sin agreed.

"Yep. My Skye does have quite the temper. Jackie seems pretty steady as long as you don't mess with her kids." Executioner shrugged his shoulders and looked at Hook. "Your girl does carry around razor blades. He's got you there, man."

"Those things were cool as shit," Pitbull added. "She gave me a few. I've got one sewn into the lining of my cut."

"Maybe they should start their own group," Bug suggested. "We'll just get them stirred up and let them loose on the population of Tenillo. I bet we'd get some results then, wouldn't we?"

"The body count would be outrageous." Kitty laughed.

"Okay, gentlemen, back to the issue at hand." Boss changed the subject back to our plans around town, and I listened with half an ear as I thought about my own plans for this weekend.

I'd gotten everything arranged with Sis, and I was ready to make my move on Brea. I'd let her stew long enough. Tonight, she wasn't going to know what hit her.

8

BREA

"I need a ride home," I confessed to Frankie.

"Shit, you and me both," Frankie was at the giddy drunk stage. I wasn't there yet, but I knew I shouldn't be driving.

"Well, you're out then," I told her as I playfully nudged her shoulder. "I'll see if Boss or Hook can take us home."

"Hook just left with Paula. I just took a shot with Boss and Jenn. Looks like you're hoofing it, sister. I'll share the spare bed with you."

"Nah, I want to go home. Well, shit. Everyone else is gone," I muttered, really not wanting to call and bother Sis for a ride when she was already settled in at home.

I'd avoided the obvious option. Chef was sitting on the couch talking to Boss right now, and I hadn't seen him take a single drink tonight. And, of course, no matter how hard I'd tried not to, I'd watched anyway. He was talking to Boss, but his eyes were on me. Again.

Chef and I had played a game of cat and mouse all night. It seemed like every time I turned my back, he somehow got behind me and touched me. They weren't intimate touches, just a brush of his fingers on mine or trailing his hand across my lower back as he passed. Earlier, when

I'd walked out of the bathroom, Chef was there in the hallway. He didn't say a word, but when I tried to walk past him, he stepped in front of me and walked me backward until I was against the wall.

The asshole never even laid a finger on me. Instead, he leaned forward and breathed on my neck for a second before he nipped at my earlobe with his teeth.

That was all. No words. Just his mouth close to my neck, so close to my mouth I could taste it, his body so close to mine that I could feel the warmth coming off of him, but nothing else. Just a little nibble on my ear and then he stepped back and walked into the bathroom. Shut the door right in my face.

Later, when I was standing behind Frankie, looking over her shoulder at something on her phone, Chef walked up behind me and molded his body against mine. He was only there for a second as he reached around us to grab a napkin out of the holder. Not a word, just a full body touch, and he was gone.

Every single time I looked up, the man was watching me.

I was about to combust.

"Brea, Chef's gonna give you a ride home," Boss said from the couch. "We'll drop your truck off sometime in the morning if you'll leave your keys on the bar."

"Oh, that's okay, Boss," I told him. "I was just about to call an Uber."

"Chickenshit," I heard Jenn whisper from her chair on

the other side of Frankie.

"Bock bock bock," Frankie started making chicken sounds and Jenn joined in.

Big hole. Right in the fucking middle of a field somewhere. They just had no idea.

"You're not taking an uber, Pickle," Chef's deep voice rang out across the room. "I've got you."

Frankie whirled around and asked, "Why do you call her Pickle?"

"Because she eats pickles all the damn time. Duh," Jenn said with a laugh.

"She does, but that's not it at all."

Jenn tilted her head and asked, "Why then?"

"Because last year, when I came back to visit, a bunch of us went to the fair together. Brea bought a pickle from one of the food trucks and walked beside me while she enjoyed the damn thing like it was her last meal on earth. I watched her eat every fucking bite, and now, every time I smell a pickle, my dick gets hard."

Boss made a sputtering sound before he leaned forward on the couch, put his elbows on his knees and his face in his hands. His shoulders were shaking with laughter, and he was making an odd wheezing sound.

"Mr. Green in the study with a lead pipe!" Frankie chortled just as Jenn took a sip of her drink. It sprayed out of her mouth, and she started coughing. Frankie, ever the good doctor, yanked Jenn's arm up and started pounding her on the back. "I got you, sis!"

Chef's expression never changed. He stared straight at me while our precious friends made asses of themselves laughing at us.

Finally, he tilted his head in the direction of the front door and asked, "You ready to go, Pickle?"

Boss started wheezing again, and Jenn's cough came back with a vengeance. Meanwhile, Frankie was using her shirt sleeve to dry her eyes while she giggled uncontrollably. I, on the other hand, was standing there like a deer in the headlights.

I'd been so horny for the last two weeks, I could barely sit still. Now, this man wanted me to hold onto him while we shot down the highway at 70mph riding a massive vibrator?

It was a motorcycle, not a vibrator. I knew that. But really?

"We'll take my truck."

"Like hell we will."

"Shit," I hissed as I reached under the counter to grab my purse. I pulled my truck keys out and slammed them down on the counter before I shot a glare at Frankie and then Jenn. They started sputtering again, and I decided to forget about the hole. I'd just leave their dead bodies out in the field for the buzzards. They'd probably give the birds indigestion. Fucking assholes. I sighed loudly and started walking toward the front door. "I'm ready."

I glanced at Chef on my way to the door and saw him

grinning. The damn buzzards could just have him too.

"I'll catch you later, Boss. Good evening, ladies," I heard Chef say from behind me before he closed the door. By the time he got off the porch steps, I was almost to his motorcycle. "Hold on, Pickle. Let me help you."

"I've been on your bike before, Chef," I grumbled as I came to a stop beside it.

I watched him throw his long leg over it and then stand it upright as he put the kickstand up. Once he had the footpegs flipped down for me, he put his hand up and I took it to balance myself as I stepped up and swung my leg over. When I tried to pull my hand away, Chef brought it to his lips. He held it there against his mouth for a long second before he kissed it and then let it go.

"Why in the hell do you have to be so nice? And so fucking persistent? Why?"

"Because I'm in love with you."

"You're a crackhead." Chef chuckled as I got adjusted in my seat and put my purse strap across my body so I wouldn't lose it on the ride. "Well, are we going?"

"See, right now, I should be calling you my little cactus. Prickly on the outside so no one can get close. But either way, you're still just my Pickle."

"Start the fucking motorcycle," I growled before I let out a loud sigh.

Chef laughed outright then, and I closed my eyes and prayed for strength. I just needed to make it home, get into my house, and have a few intimate moments with my favorite vibrator for some relief so I could finally sleep. The man was in my blood, in my head, on my last nerve, and making me fucking insane. I wavered between wanting to kill him with a sharp object or fucking him to death. Right now, the scales were balanced evenly.

Chef started up the motorcycle and I fidgeted in my seat, making sure I was sitting at an angle that kept all my good parts away from the leather underneath me. The very last thing that man's inflated ego needed was for me to have a screaming orgasm while he sped down the highway.

As if he knew exactly what I was doing, Chef let go of the handlebars and hooked his hands around the outside of my knees. He pulled me flush against him. Since he was so wide, the position spread my legs out and caused me to tilt at an angle that let me feel almost every vibration coming from the engine.

When I tried to move back, Chef turned his head and said loudly, "You move back again and I'll pull over, spank your ass, and put you right back up close to me where you belong." He yanked me up close to him again and then took his hands off my legs and revved the motor for a second as he slowly turned us around in Jenn's wide driveway. Once we were pointed at the road, he gunned the engine and we took off like a shot.

I let out a loud yell and threw my arms around his stomach to hold on. Of course, that tilted me even further forward, so now there was no escaping the vibration right there where I needed it to be. I closed my eyes and shivered.

Chef laughed loudly right before he turned onto the

asphalt and revved the motor.

"Thanks for the lift, Chef," I told him as he pulled up beside my house. "I'll see you later this week."

"Did you enjoy the ride?"

"The ride was great, thank you. Oh, you don't have to turn the bike off. I can let myself in."

"Did you *enjoy* the ride?"

I had not, to be quite honest. Somehow, every time I was close to coming, Chef had let off the gas and backed down the RPMs and left me right there on the edge. When it built back up and I was close again, he'd shift and I'd lose that hard vibration that was just about to throw me over the edge.

I was so pissed and frustrated, I could chew nails and spit out thumbtacks.

"It was perfectly pleasant, thanks," I said through gritted teeth. I stood up on the peg and threw my leg over before I hopped down. Chef had the bike settled on the kickstand before I could catch my balance, and I screamed when he leaned over and threw me over his shoulder. I started to fight him, and he slapped me so hard on the ass that I knew I was going to have a bruise. Of course, I couldn't resist wiggling again, just to make sure.

"Be still," Chef said before he slapped my ass again. "I've had just about enough of your stubbornness, little lady."

"Stubborn? You're calling *me* stubborn?" I screamed as he pushed the front door open and walked into my living room.

I was just about to freak out about my front door being unlocked when I heard my daughter yell, "Y'all have fun. See you Tuesday morning!"

I squealed as I tried to push myself up and look for my daughter. "Sis, you get your ass back in this house right now."

"Bye, Mom!"

"What the hell did you promise her to get her to go along with this, Chef? I told you I couldn't be with you. That wasn't just to protect me, that was for her too. Then you go and drag her into this . . . this scheme of yours? Really?"

"Hush," Chef ordered as he set me down on my feet just inside my bedroom. "Do you like that shirt and bra you're wearing?"

"What?" I asked, confused at the turn of the conversation.

"You heard me, Pickle. You have 10 seconds to get them off, or you're going to lose them forever."

"Like hell I will! What are you going to do with them?"

"Time's up, babe," Chef growled as he reached for my hands. He pushed them behind my back and clasped both my wrists in one of his big hands before he put his mouth on mine. When I refused to kiss him back, he pulled back a few inches and looked deep into my eyes. "Brea, you've got way too much shit swirling around in that head of yours. Let go for a little bit, and give all that to me. I'll clear it all out of your head and replace it with so many good things, you'll be walking around with your head in the clouds for the next week."

"You're gonna fuck the stress and confusion right outta me, huh?"

"I'm going to do my damndest, sweetheart."

I thought about it for about five seconds and made a decision. I'd give him this time. I'd give him until Tuesday morning. I'd let him fuck me any way he wanted, and I'd even give him a list of ideas I'd been thinking about. Once we were sated, I'd convince him that we needed to move on.

He needed a sweet woman who'd wait at home for him, and I needed a man I was positive would come home at all. Other than sexual frustration, our needs didn't match up. I was just selfish enough to want this one weekend with him to look back on later.

"You're gonna need a safe word, Pickle," Chef murmured against my neck.

"I'm gonna what?" I screeched.

"And I'm gonna need you to resist using it unless you're scared or hurting."

"Whoa, whoa, whoa." I wiggled against him and yanked my arms trying to get my hands out of his grip. "How kinky we talking here, big guy?"

"Get out of your head, Pickle. Give in. Give me this. Tell me a safe word."

Chef pulled back again until he was staring down into my eyes. He was waiting patiently for me to agree to this, but I knew that I had to say it out loud before he'd go any further.

"If we do this, you've got to promise you'll listen to me and leave me alone when we're done, okay? We'll stay friends, but you'll move on and find someone that fits in your life. I'll find some man who putters around the house in the evenings and plays golf with his buddies on Saturdays rather than gets shot at while he plays with his friends."

"I can't promise that, sugar. I can promise you I'll putter around, and I can take up golf, but I can't guarantee I'll be around until we're too old to remember our own names. I had a woman who I planned that life with, and she got sick and died, Pickle. There wasn't a goddamn thing I could do about it but love her until she was gone. You had a man like that. You made him laugh and smile every single day of his life until he died right where he wanted to be - in his house, sitting in his recliner with his wife in the kitchen, his daughter on the front porch swing, and his favorite dog in his lap. Neither one of us got that guarantee the first time, and we aren't going to get it now."

"I can't lose you too, Chef. The best way to not lose you is to never have you in the first place."

"You've already got me, Pickle, and this weekend I'm going to show you just how good I can be for you," Chef said softly before he kissed me on the lips. He pulled back, looked deep into my eyes and said, "Now. Tell me your fucking safe word."

"Sauerkraut."

9

CHEF

"Fuck me, I've been waiting on this moment for years, Pickle," I told Brea as I stared down at her from where I was standing beside the bed. "You have no idea how many times I've laid in bed stroking my cock, imagining you just like this."

"Fully dressed and trussed up like a Thanksgiving turkey? Really?"

I reached out and pinched her nipple through her shirt and her bra. Brea yelped loudly.

"Not dealing with the sass, Pickle. Not dealing with it at all tonight."

"Well, you're gonna have to gag me then," Brea said with a big smile. "I got nothing but sass, Chef."

I reached for her nipple. She tried to twist her body away from me, but her tied hands wouldn't let her get too far. I'd used a few of those scarves I'd given her to tie her wrists together before I used another to tie them to the headboard. I'd used some easy knots that would come apart with just one tug, but I hadn't told my Brea that. If I did, she'd already be on the other side of the bed yammering at me.

When I got hold of her nipple again, I held onto it. Not too tightly, but enough for her to know I had it right there between my fingers. Brea's entire body stiffened, and she got

119

still. She opened her mouth to say something sarcastic, and I raised one eyebrow to give her the chance to bite it back.

With a loud sniff, she pulled her lips in between her teeth and kept quiet.

I smiled at her and pinched her nipple anyway just so I could see her eyes get fiery and her nostrils flare as she held in whatever cuss words were dying to fly out.

I left her there, tied to the bed, and walked out of the room without a word. I went into the kitchen and found the bag I'd brought over earlier before I went to Boss's for our meeting. I got my sleep pants out and tossed them up to hang over my shoulder before I went to the refrigerator and checked to make sure Sis had picked up the items I'd asked for. There was a platter full of cheeses, deli meats, and an assortment of pickles along with two gallons of sweet tea on the top shelf. On the second shelf was another platter, this one of fruits with different dips. I'd save that for our dessert later. I had some fun things I wanted to do with the juice from those pineapple chunks.

I opened the freezer and saw the bags of Brea's favorite ice. I smiled while I filled up a big cup to feed to her while we talked. Once I had our big insulated cups filled, sweet tea for Brea and unsweet for me, I shut the refrigerator and walked back toward the bedroom. I stopped when I got to the bar and studied the tray of pastries I'd ordered and decided to share one of those with Brea now. We'd had a nice meal over at Boss's, but that was already a few hours ago. I was a big man and needed to keep my stamina up for the spitfire I had tied up in the bedroom.

Once I had everything we'd need from the kitchen, I

turned the lights off and walked into the bedroom. I set everything on the nightstand and stole a peek at Brea. She was watching my every move,

"Where are my dogs?"

"Sis has them at Frankie's until Tuesday morning."

"At Frankie's?"

"Yep. She left here and went to Boss's to pick her up, then they were going over to Frankie's to get Sis and the herd settled in."

"Frankie's in on this?"

"Yep."

"That bitch," Brea hissed out on a breath. "I knew I should have killed her."

I chuckled as I took off my shirt and tossed it over onto the chair in the corner along with my sleep pants. When I turned and looked back at Brea, her eyes were wide, and she was staring at my chest.

"Holy hell," Brea whispered as she took in every inch of my chest and arms. As her eyes went slowly down my chest, her tongue peeked out and wet her bottom lip before she bit it with her teeth. I moved my hands to the button of my jeans and slowly worked it open before I pulled the zipper down and left them hanging off my hips.

I bent forward at the waist and stared into Brea's wide eyes before I kissed her softly and then pulled away to walk over to the chair. Once I had my boots, socks, and jeans off, I slowly pushed my boxer briefs down over my hips and legs

CHEF

until I could step out of them. I put on my sleep pants and fiddled with the drawstring for a second before I slowly turned around.

Brea's mouth was hanging open now, and her eyes were on my crotch. The sleep pants did nothing to hide my erection, but that was fine. It was giving Brea quite a thrill to watch me walk toward her. Once I was right next to the bed, I stopped and readjusted my cock to a more comfortable position by my hip and then sat down next to Brea on the bed.

"I brought us a snack. How are your arms?"

"They feel fine."

"Here, have a bite, Pickle. You need to keep up your strength. We've got a long weekend ahead of us."

"You're gonna keep me tied up all weekend?" Brea asked before she opened her mouth for the bite of pastry I held between my fingers.

"Just for the really fun parts."

I fed her another bite and then took one of my own. Within just a few minutes, we'd finished our snack and I tipped her cup up for her to have a few drinks of tea.

"Now, we work on your clothes."

"Should have taken them off before you tied me up," Brea said sarcastically. "Now what are ya gonna do?'

I reached over and touched her neck for a second before I put both of my hands on the collar of her t-shirt and ripped it right down the middle. I smiled at the look of shock on her face. When she opened her mouth to yell at me, I put

122

my hand on her breast in warning, and she shut her mouth with a snap.

"I warned you," I told her as I shook my head. "I told you more than once, but you didn't listen to me. You were too busy arguing."

I took my hand off her chest and leaned over to open the nightstand drawer. I pulled out the pair of scissors I'd put there earlier and quickly cut the bra right where it connected in the middle. I tossed the scissors back into the drawer and grabbed a few pieces of ice out of the cup there and popped them in my mouth. I leaned over Brea and rested my hand on her other side as I stared down at her chest. With one finger, I pushed each bra cup off to the side.

I studied her nipples for a second, watching them get harder as the cold air hit them. Brea got turned on at the thought of what was to come. Without a word, I swooped down and sucked her nipple into my mouth. I swirled the pieces of ice around it and heard her gasp before I let it go and repeated it on the other side.

"Here, baby. Want a bite?" I asked as I reached over and grabbed a few more pieces. I dropped one into her mouth and then held another over her chest, choosing which side to start on. I decided on the left one and swirled the piece of ice I held between my fingers around her nipple until it melted, and there was water running down her side. I leaned forward and put my hot mouth where the ice had been, and Brea let out a shout. I did the exact same thing for the other side, feeding her a piece and then melting a piece on her other breast.

This time when I took the cold nipple into my mouth,

CHEF

I cupped her other breast and brought it closer so I could go back and forth between them nibbling, licking and sucking to my heart's content.

"You're so fucking beautiful, Pickle," I whispered as I worshipped her chest. "So fucking beautiful. I can't wait to see the rest of you."

"Go ahead and do that. Right now's good."

I chuckled as I watched her swallow hard and close her eyes as she tried to relax.

I pushed off with my other hand so that I was sitting next to her and then I twisted my body so I could get both hands on her jeans. Once I had the jeans and underwear over her hips, I stood up and walked to the end of the bed. I pulled off her shoes and socks and then took the jeans off one leg at a time. She was laying there in front of me wearing nothing but the pieces of her shirt and bra. Once I'd looked my fill, I picked her feet up and spread them wide so I could put my knee up on the bed between them.

I bent over and kissed my way slowly from the inside of her left knee all the way up to her bare pussy. I skipped over it and heard Brea groan as I kissed my way down to her other knee. I was kneeling on the bed between her legs now, staring down at her body. I let my gaze travel up slowly until I caught her eyes and then I winked at her.

"You can go ahead and do whatever it is you've got planned, Chef. I'm here for the duration. I'll just handle whatever you've got to throw at me until you're ready to listen to my arguments again. And I mean listen and hear me, not just blow me off." Brea closed her eyes and took a deep breath, playing the martyr like I had her trussed up ready for torture.

Well, I did have her trussed up, and I was going to torture her, but it was the best kind of torture.

"I'll just settle in then, Pickle. We seem to be at an impasse again," I told her as I laid down on my belly between her legs, my mouth inches from her pussy. "I've got nothing but time."

"You've gotta fix it." Brea gasped as she tried to lift her legs up and pull me closer. "Oh fuck."

"I'm really getting into this book, though. This is some good shit. Have you read this one before?"

"Stop reading and finish. God, let me finish."

"I mean, I know it's like a storybook happily ever after thing. I can tell that by the title of the book that the guy's a biker, right? But I had no idea the dude was gonna turn into a fucking bear. Holy shit. Now I know what you meant in the pantry. Talk about a twist. When does this guy sleep? He's ex-military, a fucking policeman, he turns into a goddamn bear, and he's *still* got time to chase this woman around and ride his bike? Jeez," I said right before I put my mouth back on her pussy and pulled her clit in between my lips. I flicked my tongue against it quite a few times and then abruptly pulled away and started reading out loud again.

"No, no, no, no," Brea whispered as she squirmed in front of me.

Randomly after one or two sentences, sometimes one or two paragraphs, I'd stop reading and put my mouth to work again. I decided to switch things up this next time, so I settled in for the long haul and switched her Kindle over to my left hand.

"Okay, so I get that he's got trust issues, I mean, who wouldn't? His family and his wife left him all because he accidentally killed that hiker? Shit. What was that fucker doing out in the woods in the middle of the night? No one is out in the woods in the middle of the night unless they're up to something. Am I right?"

Brea lifted her head up off the pillow and glared at me. While she was watching, I stuck my tongue out and flicked the tip of it against her clit a few times.

"Good grief, woman. We're gonna need to wash this blanket before we go to sleep tonight. You need a drink of tea? I think you might be getting dehydrated."

"I hate you." Brea growled.

"Now, Pickle," I whispered as I pushed one finger inside her slowly. "Don't say mean things to me."

Brea threw her head back with a groan and wiggled her hips against my hand, so I stopped my fingers forward progress. Once she was still again, I pulled back and pushed it in further as I leaned in and breathed on her clit. I was close enough to touch her clit when my lips moved, so I decided to analyze the plot line of the book we were reading for another few minutes.

"I'm wondering" kiss "if they're gonna" kiss "have that prospect" lick "turn into a bear" kiss "or maybe some other" lick "animal." kiss "Maybe a" lick "mountain lion" kiss.

"Oh God, oh God."

I slowly started fucking her with my fingers as I blew my breath out against her clit. She was so close now, I could feel her pussy rippling around me, begging for release. I was close to the edge myself. I'd been teasing Brea for almost an hour, and if I didn't get inside her, I very well might die right here between her legs. My cock was so hard, it was painful. All I wanted to do was push my way inside her until she was screaming my name and begging me for more.

I didn't know how much more I could take. Right now, Brea could barely form a coherent sentence, and I wasn't much better.

"What do I have to do, Chef? Please make it better."

"Say my name, Pickle," I whispered against her clit. "Say it sweet, and ask me nicely."

"Marques," Brea whispered. "Please, Marques, let me come."

I sucked her clit in between my lips and hummed as I fucked her with two fingers. Brea let out a shout, and I felt her clench around me as her entire body came off the bed. She was holding herself up by the ties on her hands and her feet on the mattress, pushing herself up into my face as she came with a long scream.

I devoured her, licking and sucking, pushing one finger and then two inside her steadily, pushing her for more than just one orgasm. I wanted everything she had to give and then I'd build her back up and take some more.

"Yes! Yes! Fuck yes!" Brea screamed as one orgasm rolled into another, and she hit her peak again. I twisted my fingers and found that spot inside her and rubbed it gently as I sucked on her clit. I heard her suck in a deep breath before she screamed my name until she had no more breath.

"That's what I wanted, sugar," I whispered as I slowly pulled my fingers out of her body and kissed her softly on her inner thigh. "I've been dying to hear you scream my name like that. Dying to watch you give in and let go just for a minute."

"Oh, Marques," Brea whispered as she moved her head back and forth on the pillow.

"There's more, sweetheart," I whispered as I slowly kissed my way up her body, pushing my pants down below my weeping cock. "I need more from you. I've tasted you, and now I've got to feel you."

I notched my cock at her entrance and slowly pushed in as I covered her body with mine. Brea let out a long sigh and wrapped her legs around me as I gave her some time to adjust to my size. When she started to move her hips, I let her draw me in little by little until I was seated all the way inside her.

Brea's eyes opened, and she stared into mine before she lifted her head up and kissed me. I reached up and pulled on the ties holding her hands. Her arms fell down and wrapped around my neck. As I slowly pulled out of her a few inches, I slid my hands under her body and lifted her as I sat us both up. I leaned back on my ankles and spread my knees out for balance before I thrust up into Brea's body.

Brea was worn out but wanted more, so she swirled her hips each time I pushed into her body. Our long kiss finally stopped, but her mouth was right there touching mine as we tried to catch our breath and just feel how well we fit together and how right this moment was between us.

"Tell me you love me, sugar. Just say it to me, please," I whispered against her mouth as I slowly thrust up inside her.

"Oh, Marques," Brea whispered with tears in her eyes. "I love you so much. It would be too much for me to handle if I ever lost you."

"You won't, Pickle. The risk is worth the reward. I'm yours forever and ever."

"And I'm yours."

BREA

"I never took you for a man with a bondage kink, Chef," I told him from across the bed. "This is a pretty awesome picnic, by the way. Did you choose all of this yourself?"

"I did."

"How did you know what I like?"

"I pay attention, especially when it comes to you."

"So, you're a stalker."

CHEF

Chef just grinned before he picked up another bite off the plate between us. He reached over and fed it to me and then picked up another bite for himself. When he was finished, he said, "By now, Frankie's alerted everyone that you're indisposed until sometime late Monday afternoon. Blue and Sis should be here in a few hours with dinner. She's got to pick up your dog's medicine. Apparently, Sis is doing okay away from home, but the four-legged children are not adapting as well."

"What did they do?" I groaned.

"I guess she forgot to pack their weed, and one of them's gone apeshit. I heard that right, didn't I? Your dog gets high?"

"Not high. It's CBD oil. She, well, she is a little high-strung." Chef raised his eyebrows in question, and I shrugged. "You expect us to have *normal* animals?"

"I guess you got two more dogs since the last time I saw you? Same breed?" I laughed for a second, realizing the man had no idea what he was getting into, staying in a house with me for the weekend. "Anyway, they'll be here in a little bit, but you're going to stay in the bedroom while I take care of all that."

"Oh, I am?"

"You are. If I have to tie you up again, you're gonna hate it before you love it, just like earlier."

"You can't tie me up everytime I disagree with you, Chef."

"I can't? Test me, Pickle. We're only on chapter five

of that book, you know."

I couldn't help but shiver at the thought of him reading to me, especially if he did it like he had earlier. I was almost willing to 'misbehave' just to see if he'd follow through. Almost.

10

BREA

I gasped for air as I sat up in bed, clawing at my throat as if the hands I'd felt were still there.

"Fuck! What's wrong?" Chef asked as he sat up next to me. "Did you have another nightmare? Are you okay?"

"Yeah, I'm fine," I whispered as I pushed him back to lay down. I snuggled up against his side with my eyes wide open, waiting for him to go to sleep so I could get up and go into the living room and read until I was tired again.

"Same dream every time?"

"Yeah. It's nothing, Chef. Go back to sleep. It's not even dawn yet."

I waited until I was sure he was sleeping before I crept out of bed and tiptoed into the kitchen. I set up the coffee maker and cleaned our mess in the kitchen while I waited for it to brew. By the time I had the countertops wiped down and the dishwasher loaded, there was enough coffee in the carafe to get my day started, so I made my mug and carried it out onto the porch to watch the sun rise.

I needed to get in touch with Sis today and have her bring my furkids home. I missed them dearly, and they had to be making Frankie nuts. But then again, that's what she deserved for helping Chef with this whole thing. I was still fantasizing about burying her out in the country somewhere, but what I really needed to figure out was how to handle my daughter.

Chef was one of the few people she'd connected with instantly. She got along with most everyone, but there was something about him that she'd just been drawn to right from the start. I loved the fact that the two of them were so close, but now my worry was that if something went wrong between Chef and I, my daughter would have to deal with the fallout

I didn't know how I'd deal with the fallout. I couldn't imagine how Sis would deal when it inevitably happened. His lifestyle and what he got into with our friends wasn't conducive to a long and healthy life. He'd proven that when he got shot a few weeks ago.

Since the last time Chef had visited Tenillo, he'd been on my mind. I had accepted the fact that my husband was gone and appreciated all the years we'd had together, but I had not really envisioned getting into a relationship anytime soon. I was content with my life the way it was. Until last year.

For some reason, I'd started looking at Chef in a whole new light. But he lived out of town and only visited occasionally, so it was an out of sight, out of mind situation. I wondered about him. Hell, I dreamed about him when I wasn't having my recurring nightmare, but he was not close by, so all I really had was my imagination and my vibrator.

That had been enough until the man moved home and showed up everywhere I looked. Every conversation I had with our friends, he seemed to be mentioned. I'd seen him watching me more than once, and he'd caught me watching him too. Then Jenn was attacked. Twice. The guys got shot, and we learned that Paula was a doctor before she came to Tenillo. Then she was kidnapped, and we found out that she was a badass mafia chick.

Through all of those events, Chef was right there in the middle of our group. Right where he belonged in the thick of things, and I realized that the man I'd been dreaming about lived a life that I couldn't handle. It was difficult enough to imagine the rest of the guys gallivanting around and getting shot at, but when I thought of Chef doing that, I got so tense that I could barely breathe.

Yeah, our town had more than its fair share of bad shit happen, but why did they have to be the ones to put things right? Why did they have to put themselves in the line of fire? We'd all worked so hard to get our lives back on track and find a place we could be healthy and happy, and now, they were sticking their noses into stuff that wasn't their business and getting fucking shot. Pop getting shot was horrible, and I couldn't imagine losing him. I didn't want to imagine losing any of the other guys either.

Especially Chef.

On Friday night, when he'd pulled his shirt off, I'd seen the puckered scar of the bullet's entrance. I'll admit, I was too distracted by the rest of his beautiful dark skin and rippling muscles to process much else at the time.

I shook my head and tried to focus. Just the thought of him naked was enough to make me lose my train of thought.

I took a sip of my coffee and yawned loudly. The sun

was just creeping up over the horizon now, and it looked like it was going to be a beautiful day. Since it was obvious I wasn't going to get any more sleep, I should do something productive.

"Mornin', Pickle." Chef said softly as he sat down on the step beside me. He held his coffee out so he didn't spill it as he leaned over and gave me a soft kiss. "Why didn't you go back to sleep?"

"I was just sitting out here thinking. Our weekend's almost over."

"Things have changed, babe. It doesn't have to be over."

"Nothing's changed. We had a great weekend together and I enjoyed every minute of it, but that doesn't negate the fact that I just can't be with you or anyone else."

"Explain it to me, so I can tell you how wrong you are."

"It's selfish, and I don't want to admit it out loud."

"Tell me."

"What are we doing today? What time is Sis bringing the kids home again?"

"This evening. Tell me."

"You want to take a bike ride? If I've got you for the rest of the day, we could take a ride around the lake or something."

"Maybe after you tell me your reasons, selfish or not.

Then there's something else I want to talk about."

I sighed and took a sip of coffee while I gathered my thoughts. If I didn't say something, he'd hound me until I was ready to just kill him. Stubborn ass. "Why do you and the guys have to get right in the middle of the shit that's going on around town? Why don't you let the cops deal with it? Boss is the big dog now, and he's got quite the team under him. Let them deal with it."

"Because it's our town where the people we love live, Brea. We can't just let shit go on and on, getting worse and putting people we know in danger."

"We're not in danger! Jenn got hurt because of one guy. One guy. I know y'all took care of him, and he's gone. She killed that other bitch, and the ones that took Paula got arrested."

"What about Pop? What about Skye's family? It's everywhere, Pickle. I don't want it to touch you."

"If it gets you killed, it will do more than just touch me!" I yelled. I took a deep breath and let it out slowly. "I told you before that I can't lose you. Sis can't lose you. You're one of her favorite people in the world, Chef. If I didn't know better, I'd think she was half in love with you."

"Okay, so I've got two things to talk to you about," Chef mumbled so low that I almost didn't hear him. He took a sip of his coffee and sighed before he said, "I love you. I'm gonna keep on loving you until I die. Whether that's from old age, I fall off my bike at 70 mph, someone shoots me, or you kill me yourself, I'm gonna love you until I take that last breath. Brea, I'm not going anywhere. I'm sitting right here next to you every morning until one of those things happens. I know you want me here. The last few days together cemented it."

"It was one weekend. If we work at it, we can go back to the way things were. I just can't let myself keep you, Chef. This stuff around town *has* touched my family. It scared the shit out of me when Pop got shot, but I've got to protect me and Sis, and that includes protecting ourselves from the heartbreak of ever losing you."

"You've got some serious control issues, babe. I am not opposed to finding ways to get you out of your fucking head so you can enjoy the life that's right here in front of you."

"You're not tying me up again."

"Is that a challenge?" Chef asked as he looked at me with one eyebrow raised. "I'd *love* for that to be a challenge."

"Focus."

"Just let go and let live, Pickle. I love you. You love me. I love your daughter. I'll love your herd of dogs. Fuck, I'll buy you more dogs if you want more. But I'm not going anywhere. If you still feel this strongly about us being apart, we'll talk about it again after you've given me some time to show you how good things would be."

"Like that makes any sense. Let's try this out for two weeks and then reassess?"

"I was thinking 30 years and then we'll talk about it."

"Pffft."

"What's that for?"

"You don't pay attention to a thing I say."

"I do. I really do. But when you're talking nonsense I let it drift in one ear and right out the other."

"You're not going to leave me alone about this, are you?"

"I'm not that kind of guy. You know that. I want you to look at it from an angle I don't think you've considered yet. Will you do that?"

I sighed. "Hit me."

"I loved my wife more than anything. She was my high school sweetheart that followed me off to college. She celebrated every win with me, and we mourned every loss together. Shit. When I got drafted out of college, I think she was even more excited than me. She was my biggest cheerleader and most honest critic. I loved her more every day we were together and then she died. I didn't know how in the hell I would ever move on."

"Oh, Chef," I whispered when I heard the tears in his voice.

"I had my little girl and then that went to shit, and I fucking lost her too. I was crazed, Brea, but I don't regret what I did for a second. I couldn't keep her safe like I promised her mom. I swore I'd never love anyone like I loved them. Then, one day, I was just trying to find a few minutes of fucking peace out under the stars, and instead, I found the one girl I could love just like I'd loved my own. In turn, she introduced me to the woman I thought I could never have. It opened my eyes, Brea. It opened my eyes to the possibilities just like I'm trying to open yours."

I was crying now. The tears were dripping off my chin faster than I could wipe them away. I'd never even considered that he knew exactly what I was feeling about starting over and trusting someone else with my heart.

"I left Tenillo because I couldn't watch the woman I loved be so happy with another man. Sis knew it then. She all but said so the day I told her goodbye. And now that I'm back, she's walking on fucking air at the thought that I'm gonna make her mom happy and whole again. But, really, it's you that's doing that to me, Pickle. You and Sis."

"Marques," I whispered. "I just . . ."

"Take the shot, Brea. I'll be right here beside you, loving you until my last breath."

"But . . . dammit! Why do you do this to me?"

"Make you, oh, I don't know . . . feel?"

"Yes!"

"You know heartache and pain, babe. Let's replace that with love and happiness, why don't we? Take a chance, I swear you won't regret it."

"I want you to be more careful. I know you have to do your part with the guys, but I want you to make sure this stuff doesn't touch my house or Sis. Can you promise me that nothing you and the boys do will come back on us?"

"I can promise that I'll do my best to make sure of that, but if for some reason it ever does, I'll take care of it. We'll all take care of it."

"Okay," I told him as I leaned over and nudged his

arm. He lifted it, and I scooted over so we were hip to hip as I snuggled against him. "You win. You just took the fight right out of me. I never realized you were coming from the same place I am after losing your wife and your daughter. I just never even considered it."

"When I move in here, I'd like to put their picture on the mantle."

"I'd like that. Ray's picture is up there to stay too."

"Of course."

"Hold on!" My whole body jolted when I realized what he'd just said. "When you move in?"

"Yep. Soon. Maybe next weekend."

"Give a woman a minute to adjust."

"If I do that, you'll think of 319 reasons why I shouldn't. I'm going to skip all that drama and bring my things over next Saturday. Well, more than likely, I'll start some time this week."

"You are so fucking pushy."

"I know, but you love me."

"I do."

"So, my love, tell me about this recurring dream you have."

"Nope."

"Wow. I honestly think I heard the door in your brain slam shut."

"It's got locks too."

"You're still dreaming about the kid, huh?"

"How the fuck did you know that?" I started to push my way out from under Chef's arm, but he held on tight. "I'm not talking about this!"

"You know that it had to be done, Brea. If you hadn't killed her, she'd have killed that little boy. Maybe not that day, but it would have happened."

"You don't even know what you're talking about."

"Then tell me. I know parts and pieces - stuff that I've pieced together besides what I heard you telling Blue one day."

"Killing her is not why I went back to prison, Chef."

"But it played an important part, didn't it? Explain it to me. Did you ever think that talking about it might be therapeutic enough to help you get through a whole night without having a panic attack in your sleep?"

"I don't think it would help."

"But you don't know it won't either."

"Fine." I sighed. "I guess if you're moving in, you might want to know the whole sordid tale, but I don't want you interrupting me with your sage advice. Just let me tell it. Tonight, when I have the same fucking dream, you'll see we're just wasting time here."

"I'll be quiet until you're finished. I promise."

CHEF

I looked at him skeptically, but Chef just flashed that sexy grin of his and kissed me on the end of my nose.

"I got out and did fine for a while, but when I couldn't find a job or a place to live, I got right back into the same fucking mess I'd been in before. I was high more often than not, and when I wasn't, I was chasing it. I started working with a guy I knew, and we were cooking drugs in this barn behind his house. We'd been up for days, and I finally crashed and burned. I woke up and heard this horrible screaming. It was just awful." I stopped and took a deep breath as my mind took me right back to that day. The same moment that my dreams twisted almost every night for years. "I ran out of the bedroom where I'd been sleeping, and the guy's wife was in the kitchen just beating the shit out of this poor child. He was trying to get away, but she wouldn't let him. She was gonna kill him. I tried to pull her off and give him a chance to escape, but he was too hurt to run. She went right back after him. I pulled her away again and got my arm around her neck, thinking I'd calm her ass down and figure shit out. She wasn't having it. I just wanted to help him, you know?"

"So she turned it on you?"

"With a vengeance. We fought for a while, and she was a scrappy one. She'd served time, too, and you know how it is - either know how to fight or you're nothing more than the floor they walk on."

Chef nodded knowingly.

"We were beating the shit out of each other, and she got in a good hit. Knocked me off of her, and I hit my head on the table or something. I think I blacked out for a little bit.

142

When I came to, she was kicking him. He wasn't even making a sound. So, I killed her."

"How?"

"What do you mean, how? I yanked her away and threw her on the floor. Once she was under me, I put my hands around her throat and choked her until she was dead."

"She kept fighting?"

"Oh, hell yeah, but I was beyond feeling anything by that time. That little boy was so broken that he couldn't even move his arms up to protect his face and she was just kicking the shit out of him. I wanted . . . no, I *needed* to kill her."

"So what part of that is your dream, or is it all of it?"

"In my dream, she gets the upper hand and chokes me. Then, while I'm laying there trying to catch my breath, she chokes the kid, and there's nothing I can do. That's when I wake up."

"What happened to the boy?"

"I don't know," I whispered. "I was still on top of her when the cops busted through the door. They'd had the house under surveillance for a while. The house across the road actually had cops in it, and they could hear everything somehow. They pulled me off of her, but she was already dead. They hauled me out before the ambulance even got there to look at him, but I did hear one of them say he was alive."

"Did you ever try to find him?"

"Yeah. But she was his mom. The guy I was cooking

with wasn't his biological father, and he went to prison anyway. The little boy ended up in the system, and I can't find any record of him. He'd be at least 20 by now, maybe even older. I don't know for sure. He was maybe in kindergarten or first grade. He was so fucking skinny and beat up that it was hard to guess his age, but he was tall."

"And in your dream, she's killing him after all?"

"Yeah, and I can't catch my breath to help him."

"His name never came up in your trial or anything?"

"I didn't have a trial. I had violated my parole by just being there. They gave me a drug test, and I failed it. I had to serve out my original sentence, and that was that. I wasn't ever charged with a crime for killing her."

"Cops probably thought it was a public service. It was, you know?"

"Yeah."

Chef and I sat there in silence for a few minutes until I said, "You might want to reconsider moving in with me. Sometimes, I'll go for a few weeks without having that dream, but then it starts again, and I might wake up two or three times a night. If you're in bed with me, you'll never get any rest."

"It's a chance I'm willing to take, Pickle. You're well worth some sleepless nights."

"You need a refill? My coffee's cold now."

"Yeah, I'll take one. I need some food too. Do we have any . . ."

Chef stopped talking when a truck screeched to a halt in front of my house. Soda, one of the guys that worked with Sis at the shop, jumped out and hurried up the sidewalk.

"What's wrong?" I asked, wondering if something had happened to Sis or even Pop.

"Where's Sis? She's not answering her phone, and she didn't come into work this morning. I've been waiting on her, and I just couldn't take it anymore. I tried to call both of you, too, but no one answered."

"What? Why?"

"She's off today, Soda," Chef explained. "Pop was supposed to tell you guys that she stayed at a friend's house over the weekend, and she'll be back at work tomorrow morning."

"Oh shit," Soda mumbled as he ran his hands over his face and back over his short black hair. "When I talked to her last night, she was distracted because there was a lot of noise with the television on and the dogs all over the place. She didn't say anything about not coming in this morning. I guess she thought I knew."

"You talked to her on the phone last night?"

"Babe, there was something else I wanted to talk to you about this morning, and I was just about to get to it," Chef interrupted.

"Why did you talk to her on the phone last night, Soda?"

Soda was one of Pop's trusted employees who lived

out on the compound and had taken over running everything along with Sis after Pop got shot. He was at least 40 and had been out of prison for five or six years. Sis had been working with him since he came to Tenillo freshly paroled, and I knew that the two of them had become good friends over the years.

What I didn't know was that they talked on the phone on their days off and at night, and there was something more going on.

I studied the man in front of me, looking at him from an entirely different viewpoint than I ever had. He was tall, probably at least 6'3". His skin was a beautiful shade of golden brown - not quite as dark as Chef's. He had short hair and a well-kept beard.

Right now, he looked relieved but stressed out. His big brown eyes were searching mine as if he didn't quite know what to say. I watched the muscles in his arms flex over and over again as he nervously opened and closed his hands. Soda had always had a few quirks and occasionally came off as a nerd on certain subjects, but he was a really good guy. A really nice, muscled, tattooed, hard-working guy.

I'd never noticed before, but Soda was a damn good-looking man.

And at the moment, he was standing in my front yard completely freaked out because he couldn't get in touch with my daughter. He was way more upset than a co-worker would be if someone didn't show up for their shift.

He was worried like a boyfriend would be if he couldn't find his beloved girlfriend.

"Holy shit," I whispered as it hit me.

146

"Pickle? You okay?"

"I'm in love with your daughter, Brea. I'm sorry this is how you had to find out. I've been telling her for a while that we needed to come clean, but she wanted you settled and happy first."

"Holy. Shit."

"Brea? Are you okay?"

"My daughter's got damn fine taste in men," I observed, mostly under my breath, comparing Soda to Chef. "Apparently, we have a type."

Chef threw his head back, and his laughter boomed, but Soda just looked uncomfortable.

"Soda, let me go inside and get my phone. I'll give you the number of the friend she's staying with, and you can get in touch with her that way, okay?" Soda nodded, and I turned to Chef. "This is the part where I make myself scarce, and you scare the living shit out of the man while you explain to him how he should treat my daughter."

"I've already done it, Pickle. He's been sufficiently traumatized."

"Not just by Chef either," Soda grumbled. He nodded his head curtly, then looked at me when he said, "Although, if terrifying threats were a competition, he and Hook took the top spots. Preacher is solid in third place."

I watched Soda shiver, and I almost felt sorry for the guy.

"Does everyone know except for me?"

"Kind of like how everyone knew I was in love with you before you realized it? Pretty much. I don't think the girls know, if that's any consolation."

"Well, that probably just saved their lives. They've been inches away from unmarked graves for a few days now."

CHEF

"I told you that you'd do fine, man," I reminded my grinning student over our video conference. "You just had to step back for a minute and get your head on straight. Keep that shit in mind as you go on to whatever magic you plan to do with your life."

"Good advice. I was terrified I was going to fail, but you and your buddies really helped me out that night by getting my mind off of things. Thanks, Dr. Green."

"Of course. You keep in touch, man. Either hit me up by email or find me online, and we'll team up and play together again. Okay?"

"I will. Bye, Dr. Green."

I watched the screen blink out and reached up and turned the camera off before I shut my computer down for the day. I'd had five different tutoring sessions with students today, and my brain was tired.

When I'd started this online tutoring venture, I really didn't think there would be much interest. I just wanted a chance to connect with students again after I'd been released from prison, and Preacher had helped me get everything set up. The amount of responses was insane, and I'd had to pick and choose students before I wore myself too thin.

The website Preacher had created for me was almost

useless now. Somehow, I'd gotten on the radar of some very important, very rich families who wanted their kids to succeed and were willing to pay dearly for my time. Those rich families told their friends who also had children going to elite schools around the country, and my student base was set. I made sure that for every two paying students, I took in at least one student who couldn't afford me but had asked for my help.

With the classes I was teaching at the college here in town and the students I already had on my roster, I was putting in at least 50 hours a week and loving every minute of it. There was just something about seeing that light come on in their eyes when they *finally* grasped what had been giving them trouble. It was what I'd loved about teaching, and that feeling of accomplishment never got old.

Although, I would admit that the online thing was much better than having a classroom of high school students staring at me like I was the dumbest adult on the planet and giving me shit at every turn.

"Another successful elitist has ventured forth from the womb of his privileged upbringing and will now take his place in the upper crust of society because of our Chef," Preacher said sarcastically. "Isn't that just sweet?"

"He's just as important as the kid I'm tutoring who goes to a community college in Montana, Preach. They're all just kids to me."

"Kids that can pay you money."

"No doubt, but if some of them didn't, I wouldn't be able to help the ones that can't too."

"Are you finished for the day? Wanna go for a ride?" Santa asked from the couch where he'd been napping for the last hour. "This last trip stressed me the hell out. Apparently, there's some fool hitting a bunch of retail stores around Phoenix. Asshole apparently thinks he's as good as I was back in the day. I gave nine consults in two days before I flew home last night, and by the time I got off the plane, every single one of them had emailed me a list of fucking questions and wanted contracts."

"Are Bug and Kitty just as busy?"

"They are. Bug got a contract with a chain of banks who lost a shit ton of their archived records in a fire. He's working on 16 buildings right now. He's gonna end up pulling his hair out if his contact with their corporate office doesn't get off his ass. The man needs to go for a ride. We should call him. Kitty too."

"Get him over here, and let's go out for a while. Brea's at the office working on the books. All I've got left here is my computer equipment, and I'd like to get that moved tonight. I think Soda's going to do it for me. He's been sucking up to Brea every chance he gets since he told her about he and Sis, and that flattery and bootlicking includes me somehow."

"How's living with Brea working out?" Santa asked as he sat up and ran his hands through his hair.

"I almost forgot! I bought you some noise cancelling ear plugs, man," Preacher told me as he stood up and started for the door. "I'll get them."

Santa and I watched Preacher hurry outside to go over to his house, and I just shook my head.

"I've never understood what the deal is with him and the girls. Why does he get so fucking irritated when they show him any attention?"

I shrugged and looked at my friend. "I think he just doesn't really know how to take them. The man went to prison when he was just a kid, all because of a girl. I think that fucked him up somehow."

"He's fucked up, that's for sure. Him and Frankie ended up yelling at each other on the porch at Hook and Paula's the other night after dinner. I thought she was going to choke him to death."

"Chef!" I heard Sis yelling from outside right before she flung open my screen door and rushed into the house. "You've got to come see what Pop and I found!"

I stood and stared at Sis who was gesturing excitedly toward my front door.

"Santa! You come too! I need muscles. I want to explore, but I can't get the door open."

"What did you find, Sis?" Santa asked as he stood too.

"There's a big metal door in the ground. We almost walked right over it when we were out checking on the goats."

"There's a big metal door *in the ground*?" I asked her, sure I was confused somehow. "Or there's a building out there?"

"Come look! Come on, Preacher!" Sis said excitedly as she tugged on my hand and dragged me past Preacher who'd just walked back inside. "I want to get inside and see what's down there!"

I let Sis drag me out of the house, and I heard Preacher and Santa walking behind us. Pop pulled up in his golf cart that he'd modified into an ATV and cut the engine just as we got out to the road that led back through the junkyard to the fields beyond.

"Take this. It's quite a distance. I'm parched, so I'm gonna let Sis show you what we found. When you get it open, come back and get me. Me and the girl discovered it together, so we get first dibs on exploring it."

"Alright, Pop," I told him with a laugh. "We'll make sure we don't leave you out."

Preacher furrowed his brow. "A metal door in the ground? That's got to be a bunker. It's the government. They're tunneling around under us since satellites make it harder to hide their shit now. I knew it!"

"Preacher," Santa said with a sigh as he got into the passenger seat of the ATV. I turned and watched Sis and Preacher settle onto the bench seat in the back before I squeezed myself down into the driver's seat and started up the engine. "I sincerely doubt that the government is tunneling underneath us. You're toeing that crazy line in the sand again."

I let Sis direct us to the spot where she and Pop had made their discovery. There was a long stick poking out of the ground, and Pop had tied one of his red bandanas on it like a flag so that it was easy to see.

We pulled up close to the marker, and I shut the

CHEF

engine off and pried myself out of the little machine. Sis had hopped off the back before we even came to a complete stop and was kneeling down in the grass. When I got closer, I realized there was a concrete pad about six inches high that was camouflaged by the tall grass. I stepped up on it and looked down at the circular metal disc that Sis was crouched on.

"What the hell?" I asked aloud to no one in particular.

"I told you it was government shit!" Preacher crowed as he scuffed his boot on the faded paint of a military emblem. "Tunneling right the fuck under us. There's probably scientists down there who haven't seen daylight in years."

"We're still on Pop's land, aren't we?" Santa asked as he slowly turned around in a circle and looked at the fields surrounding us.

"Yeah, he had a surveyor come and mark the property lines not too long ago. You can still see the orange markers over there," I pointed into the distance. "He's planning on building some more houses out here."

"But there used to be a military base right over there. What if these tunnels go from there to somewhere else?"

"Shit," I whispered. "Okay, Sis. Hop up for a minute so we can reassess."

"What's there to reassess? It's a government bunker. I told you!" Preacher huffed.

I stared at him until he calmed down some and then looked over at Santa as Sis stood up and walked over to the ATV to sit.

"Pop's property or not, this is government shit. We are not the shining sons of said government, and if we get caught fucking with their shit, we might just become their guests in a prison on an island somewhere. I say we keep a lid on this until we've talked to Boss and maybe gotten Sin and his guys in on it. We'll figure out where to go from there. As far as I'm concerned, we just pretend we never saw this thing and move on, but I'd imagine more investigation should be done."

"We bring in those shining sons of the government and let them help us if we decide to try and go down there," Santa agreed.

"Oh, I'm going down there," Preacher assured us. "I want to see everything. I've been waiting my whole life for a moment like this. There's probably a research facility down there or maybe a nuclear reactor."

I closed my eyes and took a deep breath, but I heard Santa chuckle.

"Holy shit! Those fucking cats Boss found are *huge*, and they came from somewhere out here. Three words: nuclear fucking testing."

I let my head fall forward, and my chin hit my chest. Santa laughed outright and slapped Preacher on the back before he said, "Yeah, Preach. They're doing animal testing on feral kittens to see if they can make them go all Hulk smash. Then they can train them to invade other countries."

"You guys always have to take it too far and make it sound crazy."

"We take it too far? We do?" I asked with wide eyes.

"Really?"

"Oh, fuck both of y'all. I'm going down there, dammit."

"Let's go with Chef's suggestion for now, brother. Maybe we can find a way to get you a tour of the underground facility without all of us getting thrown into Guantanamo."

***

"Okay, let's see what we've got out there while there's still some daylight," Sin told our group before he held the door open for us to walk outside. "You got Pop and Sis settled about this?"

"Neither of them are happy about it, but I promised that if we didn't find anything dangerous, we'd take them out there in the next few days."

"I'm sure it's nothing. Probably just some bunker the government built and abandoned. They do that," Phantom said with a dark laugh.

"I swear, it amazes me that some of them are in charge of shit. I was locked up with a guy who should have been released months before, but they lost his records. I don't just mean the file in the office, I mean they lost his whole fucking record somehow. It took an act of God for them to finally release him." Kitty shivered dramatically and said, "Imagine having to spend months in prison when you didn't have to just because they lost your paperwork."

"That sounds like the military." Saint laughed. "Just

like the military."

"Bureaucratic bullshit. I'm knee deep in it every day in the office," Boss complained.

"Has shit calmed down some since that woman's not working there anymore?" Kitty asked Boss.

"Some. At least in the office itself. I'm still surrounded by men I don't know if I can trust or that I wouldn't trust if my life depended on it. Fuck. One of my detectives is a boil on the ass of humanity, but he's so slippery that I can't catch him fucking up so I can get rid of him."

"Is he the one working the missing girls' cases?" Sin asked.

"He was. I pulled him off of them, but he sniffs around all the time. It's making Wrecker fucking nuts. He's gonna just end up killing the man before this shit is over, especially after last night," Boss explained. "Three more girls went missing. Just gone without a trace. No one saw them get taken, no one heard them scream for help . . . nothing. Their cars ended up at some random place with everything intact just like they got out and walked off the face of the earth."

"So these disappearances happen in spurts?" Preacher asked.

"That's exactly what's been happening. Just when we think we've got a lock on things and can revise our tactics, it stops completely. We've got people working in all the surrounding counties, and I've got word to every agency in Texas and the neighboring states on what to watch for so we can put all our data together, but that doesn't do anything more than create more goddamn paperwork."

"How many women now?" I asked.

"Including the girls that went missing last night, we're up to 15 in Tenillo alone. If you add the cases in the surrounding counties, we're in the high 30s, man. There's still some that haven't even gotten back to me yet. There's mention of the FBI coming in if we can prove that these are all connected."

"How much fucking data does the FBI need to prove they're connected? Damn."

"It's the fucking government, Chef. They move at their own pace."

"Okay, here we are," Santa told our group. "Kitty, this is why we brought you. What do you think it would take to get into this thing?"

Kitty walked over to the platform and set the bag he was carrying down by his feet. Phantom stepped up beside him and then both men squatted down and talked softly for a few minutes, nodding occasionally as they talked about the technicalities of how to break into the lock.

"I'm just going to throw this out there. I mentioned it earlier, but I have a few questions. Why do we give a shit what's under there?" I raised my voice to talk over Preacher's objections. "And I mean other than Preacher's reasoning. And are we really sure a bunch of ex-cons should be fucking with government property?"

"Technically, it's on Pop's land," Santa pointed out.

"If it's got their fucking name on it, it's their property."

"Chef, my friend, you're the most careful, patient, and methodical man out of your entire club. How in the hell did you get caught for whatever it was you did?" Saint asked me.

"I stayed to watch," I admitted. "I wanted to make sure they were all dead."

Saint's eyebrows rose, and I could tell he didn't know why I'd gone to prison.

"After my wife died, my daughter turned to drugs and got connected with this low-life pimp that kept feeding them to her as long as she did what she was told. I tried over and over again to tear her away. I even sent her to rehab twice, but he had as much hold over her as the fucking drugs. The last time she ran to him, she OD'd in the back room of his house, and it took three fucking days for him to call in the authorities to get her body. I very *carefully* created a toxic smoke bomb and then watched his house and *patiently* studied his movements. I then *carefully* tossed the canister into his house through a window and *methodically* counted every man who crawled out. Then I very *patiently* watched them die. I wanted to make sure I didn't miss a single one. By the time the last one died, the cops were there."

"Fuck," Saint whispered.

"As far as I'm concerned, they should have given you a medal instead of jail time." Sin told me.

I grinned. "A jury found me not guilty on 14 charges of first-degree murder, but convicted me of misuse of state property because I made the bomb in the science lab at the high school where I taught chemistry."

"Holy shit," Saint chuckled. "That's just so . . . "

"Diabolical?" Santa mumbled.

"Petty misuse of government time by a DA with a tiny dick?" Preacher added. "And Chef's quite possibly certifiably insane?"

"Maybe a little bit of all of those," Saint agreed.

I shrugged my shoulders and looked over at Kitty and Phantom. "If there is something down there, who are we going to call?"

"Ghostbusters!" Pitbull cheered. Sin slowly turned and stared at his friend for a few seconds before he looked back at me and shook his head.

"If there's not anything interesting, and it's just a dusty old bunker, we've gotta go get Sis and Pop and let them see. I promised them a chance."

"We will, just not until we know it's safe," Boss assured me.

"Unless it's bolted on the inside, we've got the lock open," Kitty called out.

"Ninja badasses with years of experience in this kind of shit, would you like to go down the hatch first?" Boss asked Sin and his men with a grin.

Sin shrugged and said, "Sure. Why not?"

"Are you listening to him, Sis?" I whispered so I didn't interrupt Boss as I leaned close to Sis and nudged her with my shoulder.

Sis sighed and nodded.

"It's not safe for you, honey. I need you to stay out of the field and close to the buildings until we tell you otherwise, okay? The world's a crazy place, and I worry about you."

"I know."

"Remember when I left years ago, and I told you I didn't want anything to happen to you?"

"Yeah."

"That still applies. I don't know what I'd do if something happened to you, sweetheart."

"You'd probably go on a killing spree."

"I bet every single man in this room would."

"Mom taught me how to gamble, Chef, and that's a sucker bet if I've ever heard one."

12

BREA

"Hello, beautiful," Chef whispered as he stepped up behind me and wrapped his arms around my waist. "Turn the burner off."

"What? Why?"

"Because I need a minute, and I don't want you to burn something." I turned the burner down so the sauce could simmer and then twisted in Chef's arms so I could face him. I looked up at him just as he leaned down to kiss me. "Dance with me."

Lauryn Hill's version of "Can't Take My Eyes Off of You" had just started on the stereo, and I smiled at Chef as he started to move to the music. I moved my arms up around his neck as we swayed and leaned my head to the side when Chef started nibbling on my neck.

Chef pulled his head back at the same time he pushed me away from him. He grabbed my hand and twirled me around a few times until my back was to his front and then he leaned down and started nibbling on the other side of my neck as our hips moved together.

When that song ended, one of my favorites from my playlist started, and Chef spun me around again and pulled me into his arms. While Pink sang "Walk Me Home", Chef danced me around the kitchen and even dipped me when the song was over.

As he pulled me up, the back door opened and our two Frenchies, Ripley and Danee, came running through the house followed by Sis who had her possum and hedgehog snuggled together in a scarf she used as a carrier for them.

"Is dinner ready?" Sis asked as Chef held me in his arms.

"Well, hello to you too," I said sarcastically as I watched her stir the sauce on the stove.

"She's still mad at me," Chef explained. "I told her she can't go exploring at Pop's for a while."

Sis gave Chef side eye, but didn't say anything, letting me know that he'd guessed correctly on his first try.

"You can make a plate. Everything's ready," I told my daughter. "You gonna get over your snit anytime soon?"

"It's not a snit, I just want to know why."

"Because the guys went down there and realized that someone's been using that tunnel recently," Chef admitted. "It wasn't us, and there's no good reason for anyone to be traipsing around under there unless they're doing something illegal. If that's the case, the last thing I want is for you to drop down in there, interrupt some bad shit, and get hurt or killed because of it."

Sis snorted. "You couldn't just tell me that earlier?"

"It's not enough for me to just ask you not to do something?"

"She likes an explanation," I explained with my eyebrows raised in warning.

"Lesson learned," Chef conceded as he waited for Sis to turn around and acknowledge him. After she'd finished making her plate, she twisted around and gave him a dazzling smile before she walked back out of my house toward her own. "Damn, she's sassy. I wonder where she gets it."

"If it's a bad quality, I just say she got it from her father's DNA. All the good shit came from me."

"You never told me what happened to him? Were y'all married? Does she visit him?"

I slowly shook my head. "Not married. He didn't want shit to do with her, so she didn't want shit to do with him. He died a few years ago, and she was his only living relative. We found that out when a lawyer called to tell us she was rich."

"How'd he die?"

"He got drunk, tripped over his own feet, bumped his head, and drowned in a stock tank while he was checking cattle on his ranch. Couldn't have happened to a nicer man." Chef's laughter was so loud that Ripley jumped and started barking at him. She started zooming around the couch, bouncing on the furniture as she ran. "Time for her medicine."

"What the hell?"

"She gets it twice a day, or she acts like *that* all the time," I explained as I reached into the cabinet for her meds.

Once I'd given them to her, it was just a waiting game until they kicked in. "Are you hungry?"

"Starving. Oh, you mean for dinner? Sure, I could eat."

I shook my head as Chef grinned wickedly. Once our plates were made, we walked out onto the back porch to eat.

"Now, tell me about this tunnel Sis stumbled across. I'm sure Preacher had to be sedated when he found out."

I choked on my tea laughing at her comment. "He almost did. He's convinced there's nuclear testing going on out there now."

"Of course he is. You think it's dangerous for her to be out there?"

"The guys went in and realized that others had been there recently, so I'm not sure what the next steps are going to be."

"You could get Preacher to hunker down in there to wait until someone comes through," Brea suggested. "Nah. I'd miss him."

"You would not."

"I would. Okay, maybe I'd miss teasing him."

"That's more like it. Do you think Sis is going to forgive me?"

"Did you hear that?" Brea asked as she tilted her head and looked out into the yard with an alarmed expression.

"Hear what?"

"Shhh."

I listened but could only hear the breeze blowing the leaves and one of the neighbors doing something in their yard. Just then, I heard a woman scream.

I put my plate on the table and stood as I stared out into the yard.

"You heard it too?" Brea asked quietly as she stood up beside me.

There was another scream followed by a long string of Spanish words and another scream.

"That came from Sis's house," I told Brea as I started for the screen door.

Sis lived in a small two-bedroom mother-in-law cottage at the back of Brea's property. It was just far away enough for privacy but close enough for comfort. After that third scream, I couldn't get there quickly enough. I banged on the door just as Brea punched in a code. She pushed the door open, and we stood there, completely stunned.

Sis was sitting at her kitchen table eating dinner, and there was a huge yellow parrot sitting on a perch in front of her. He was holding a carrot in one claw, and it was halfway up to his mouth for a bite. Sis had a bite of food on her fork with her mouth open, staring at us.

"Shut the door!" Sis yelled just as the parrot dropped his treat and launched himself off his perch.

The bird was coming right at us, trying to escape

through the open door. Brea squealed and ducked, but I stood there hoping to block its exit. The bird realized I wasn't going to move too late to change direction and smacked right into my chest. He fell down on Brea's back and got tangled in her hair.

Sis was screaming as she ran across the room to rescue the bird, Brea was screaming because the bird was going crazy on her back, and the bird was screaming a litany of Spanish words that I recognized as some of the filthiest language possible.

Sis finally got the bird settled on her arm and started walking it back toward its perch, and I leaned down to help Brea up off the floor.

"What. Is. That?" Brea growled at her daughter.

"It's a walrus," Sis answered with a straight face.

"Why is it here?"

"And why is it cussing in Spanish?" I asked, confused.

"He is not an it. This is Rodrigo. He's a parrot," Sis explained slowly, as if Brea and I really believed it was a walrus rather than a bird who'd just insulted my mother in a foreign language. "He's a little dramatic and high strung."

"Did he just call me a stupid bitch?" Brea fumed.

"I need to google a list of Spanish swear words, but yeah, I think so," Sis said softly as she stared at the foul-mouthed bird. "He calls me lots of things, but he's never called me that."

"I'm gonna kill Hook."

I bit back a laugh and stared at the floor for a second while I tried to hold it together. I gently reminded her, "It could be worse. Paula is learning how to live with a tiger right now."

Brea slowly turned and glared at me.

"Hook didn't give him to me. Soda did. He was an anniversary gift."

Brea turned back to look at her daughter. Without another word, she walked past me out the door, headed back to her house.

"Bye, Chef. You have fun with that," Sis teased.

"Shit," I growled before I followed after Brea. She was halfway back to the house already, but I caught up and grabbed her arm. I spun her around until I was holding her in front of me and smiled before I asked, "What's got you so riled?"

"How is all of this going on right under my nose, and I don't realize it? First, I find out she's dating Soda, and now, I discover they've been together long enough for an anniversary?"

"It's not been that long, Brea. They tiptoed around each other for years until he finally got the guts to ask her out about six months ago."

"See? Why did I not know that?"

"She's got a life, Pickle. Not sure what to tell you."

"And another thing, can we not have a *normal* pet in this family?"

"That's highly unlikely. You have a dog that runs around like a crackhead unless you get him high and a hedgehog that thinks a possum is his soulmate. You guys passed normal ages ago. Did you get enough to eat?"

Brea let out a dramatic sigh but didn't so much as blink at my change of subject. "I need to get started on the dishes."

"Nope," I said curtly before I bent at the waist and lifted Brea over my shoulder. "Time for bed, Pickle."

"It's not even eight o'clock!"

"Didn't say it was time for sleep, just said it was time for bed."

Brea instantly stopped struggling. I could hear the laughter in her voice when she said, "In that case, put me down, and I'll race you."

I heard Brea gasp for air just as she sat up in bed. I gave her a second to realize she was awake before I reached out and rubbed her back to soothe her. This was the first nightmare in almost a week, but she'd warned me that they came and went.

"Come here, Pickle," I whispered as I pulled her back to lay in the crook of my arm. I listened as her breathing slowed, and she relaxed against me.

One thing I'd learned within our first few nights together was that Brea wouldn't go back to sleep after a dream. She'd get up and putter around the house rather than let herself fall back to sleep and risk having another nightmare.

But . . . I'd found something that helped her sleep again.

I turned my body so that we were facing each other and reached up with one hand to cup her cheek before I gave her a soft kiss. She kissed me back, and her hand drifted down my stomach and underneath the waistband of my sleep pants to wrap around my cock. I was instantly hard for her, and I heard her soft laughter as I kissed down her neck to her shoulder blade.

Brea let go of me and pulled her hand up to push at my shoulder. I let her have her way and ended up on my back with her slowly kissing her way down my chest and stomach until she reached my hip and nipped me with her teeth. She pushed the waistband of my pants down until my cock was free, and in the next second, wrapped her lips around the head while she held it at the base.

I gasped and my hips came off the bed. Brea pulled her mouth back and giggled.

"Maybe it's time I tie *you* up for a little torture, Mr. Green."

"Oh no." I stuttered out a laugh as her tongue came out and licked around the head of my cock. "No ties for me."

Brea worked her mouth as far down as she could - I felt the tip touch the back of her throat. She wrapped her hand tight around the base and stroked me as she took as much into her mouth as she could over and over again.

Within seconds, I was on the edge, whispering for her to crawl over me and take me inside her.

"Let me play for a little while," Brea whispered before she took me all the way into her throat again. "I want to see how long you can take it."

"Not long," I admitted. "Not long at all."

"Oh, it's very long. And thick too," Brea murmured as she stroked me from the base to tip and ran her thumb over the top. "I like it. I like what you do with it too. I love how it feels when you're inside me, when you lose control and just slam into me."

"That's gonna happen sooner rather than later, Pickle. You keep touching the back of your throat with my cock, and it's gonna happen right the fuck now."

Just to test me, Brea pushed her face down over my dick, got it to the back of her throat, and swallowed. It squeezed the tip so perfectly that I let out a shout and grabbed the hair on either side of her head. I wasn't sure if I wanted to pull her off me or hold her there for her to do it again.

I realized I was pulling her hair, so I let go. She never stopped moving her head up and down but reached out with one hand to pull mine back into her hair. She put her hand on top of mine and pushed it down as if she was directing me to guide her head.

I damn near came in her mouth at the thought of her letting me direct her, and I guess she knew that when she suddenly got still. She kept her mouth on me but stopped moving, waiting for me to direct her.

"Fuck," I muttered as I pulled her head up and then pushed her down again. I lifted my head up so I could watch and groaned when I started moving her up and down in the perfect rhythm. I took it as long as I could before I yanked her off my cock so I could catch my breath. "I can't take anymore, or I'm gonna come. Sit on my face, or let me fuck you. Your choice."

Brea scrambled up the bed until she was on her hands and knees beside me. Without a word, I moved behind her. I ran my fingers through her heat and realized she was wet and ready, so I positioned myself and slowly started to push my way in.

"I thought you said you were gonna fuck me," Brea growled as she shoved her body back, taking me all the way inside her with one push.

"You want it like that, do you?" I reached up and wrapped her hair around my hand and tugged. "I can give it to you like that, sugar."

I set my hips in motion, tugging on Brea's hair to bring her body back toward mine on every forward stroke. Within seconds, she was moaning as loud as I was, and I could feel her muscles gripping me, preparing for her orgasm. I let go of her hair and pushed her shoulders so that she was facedown in the bed, giving me more room to slide in at a different angle.

I had barely gone three more strokes when Brea screamed and clutched at the sheet beside her. Within seconds, I joined her, letting out a shout as I came deep inside her body.

With a grunt, I fell forward on top of Brea, and her legs slid down so that she was flat on the bed beneath me. We were still connected, and I moved my hips back and forth a few times before I stilled.

"You're not even hard, and you could still fuck me like this," Brea mumbled. "I'm just gonna throw away all my toys."

I pushed up with my arms so I wouldn't crush her as I slowly started fucking her again. I wasn't a young guy, I was damn near 50 years old, so the odds of me going again anytime soon were slim, but feeling her walls quivering around my cock still felt magical even though I was soft inside her. Brea let go of the sheet with one hand and slid it under her body. I heard her moan as she touched herself, and amazingly, I felt my cock start to get hard again.

I pulled out of her body and moved over to the side so I could turn her. When she was on her side, I lifted her top leg up and straddled the one on the bed. I pushed back into her body as I lifted her leg up over my shoulder.

With just the faint light coming in through the blinds, I could watch her touch herself in this new position and see the look on her face. She was relaxed now with a dreamy smile on her lips, and she moved her fingers lazily over her clit as I slowly fucked her.

All too soon, her hand started moving faster and so did I. Before long, we were coming together again. I held myself inside her and felt her inner muscles contract when she laughed softly.

"You gonna just stay inside me until we work up to

another one?"

I slowly pulled my hips back until I was out of her body and heard her moan as she flopped over to her back.

"Stay just like that, Pickle, and I'll clean you up," I whispered as I leaned forward and softly kissed her lips.

Brea made a soft sound, and I knew she was almost asleep. I got out of bed, cleaned myself with a wet rag in the bathroom, and then took a warm wet rag back into the bedroom to take care of my girl. By the time I got back, she was sleeping deeply, and I took care not to wake her as I cleaned her up as well as I could. I tossed the washrag into the hamper and then adjusted the sheet and blanket over my woman before I crawled into bed and pulled her body close to mine.

Lucky for me, the way I'd found to relax her back to sleep worked for me too. Just before I let sleep take over, I tilted my head down to kiss her forehead and whispered, "Love you, Pickle."

Even in her sleep, she answered me. "My Marques. Love you."

13

BREA

"Sis needs me to meet her at the store," I told Blue as I dropped my phone into my purse. "Want to come?"

"Sure," Blue said with a shrug as she stood up from the table. "What is she needing?"

"That fucking bird Soda got her needs some toys," I grumbled. "Is there a bird toy section at Walmart that I've missed?"

"That bird needs Rosetta Stone, not toys. The other day when I came over and you weren't here, I walked back to see Sis, and that little bastard cussed me out in Spanish *and then* he cussed me out in English too! Does he know how to say anything but vulgarities?"

"You know, that's the first time I've heard you complete an entire thought without using the word 'fuck' like a comma. Have *you* been using Rosetta Stone?'

"Fuck you," Blue growled as she pulled open the door of her truck.

Once we were on the road, I asked my old friend about her future. "What brought you back to Tenillo? You still haven't told me."

"A man. Of course."

"Did you follow one, or are you running from one?"

"I don't run. It's not in my DNA," Blue told me with a laugh as she turned onto the access road so we could get on the highway and head across town. "If I tried to run, my thighs would rub together so hard that I'd start a fire."

"Whatever," I grumbled. "You'd run if it was necessary."

"Can't think of any reason it would be necessary. Not a single one."

"So, tell me about this man."

"I thought it was the real deal. Everything seemed to be going just fine. We'd been seeing each other for about a year, and things were progressing nicely. I only wanted to kill him when I had to listen to him chew, and I could get around that by leaving the television on while we ate."

"Well, at least you found a solution."

"You know how I hate that."

"So was he cheating? Did he lie? Talk to me."

"He hit me."

"And then you killed him?"

"No. I realized he'd been building up to that since the day I met him. It was a gradual thing, you know? I didn't see it as it happened, but after he did it, he said, 'I didn't mean to, but you just made me so fucking mad.' I stood there in the bathroom staring at my blackening eye and realized he'd just been working up to it, you know?"

"Yeah, I know. Some of them are devious like that."

"I realized while I was staring at my reflection, wondering how in the hell I was going to hide my black eye so I could go to work, that we'd been headed for that moment for a while. I almost thought that maybe I had deserved it because I was arguing with him about something completely stupid."

"Oh, hell no! There is no fucking reason . . ."

"I know!" Blue interrupted me. "I know. I'm just saying that he had me so fucked up that I found myself wondering if it was my fault. I looked back at disagreements we'd had before and realized he'd convinced me that I was always wrong. I'd even apologized for shit that was not my fault at all."

"That happens, Blue. No woman walks into a relationship thinking it's okay to get knocked around. What did you do to him? I know you didn't let it lie."

"I was staring at my reflection while he was unconscious in the bathtub," Blue admitted. "I honestly thought about drowning him, but I resisted. Instead, I hurried and packed up all the shit I had there and went to my place. All I could think was that I wanted to get away from him."

"Did he follow you?"

"Not that night, but he broke into my apartment a few weeks later and trashed the place. Luckily, I had taken Granny, the girls, and all my equipment with me to one last appearance I had scheduled, so they were fine. Since I had my equipment with me, he didn't break *everything*, just what I hadn't already packed up to move."

"Is he going to come looking for you?

"I don't think he'd do that, but he's still calling day and night and sending me text messages. Depending on his mood, they're sweet and apologetic or more of the 'I'm gonna find you and kill you' variety."

"Let that fucker try," I growled.

"The night after I got back from the conference, I had me and the girls all packed up and we came home. Considering he'd ripped apart or smashed all of my furniture, packing wasn't a chore."

"Does your brother know about this guy?" I asked. Blue shook her head, and I sighed. If he found out, he'd lose his damn mind, and it would take an act of God to keep him from killing the man. "I'm glad you're back, Blue. Are you ready to move into your new place?"

"I am. I've got my new job that I like working for Pitbull at the Infidels bar. My vlog is getting so much traffic that I might be able to do that for a living someday. Our house will be ready next week, and Granny will move into her tiny house behind mine as soon as the renovations are finished. The girls are healthy and happy, and so am I. That bastard's in my rearview, and I'm ready to move forward."

"There's Sis," I told Blue as I lifted my hand and pointed toward my daughter's car on the other side of the parking lot. "Who is she talking to?"

"She looks uncomforta . . ." Blue started to say something before we both yelled when we saw the man in front of Sis start to drag her over to his car.

Blue hit the gas and started to speed toward Sis, but a car pulled out of its parking place, and she had to slam on the brakes. She laid on the horn, and the car lurched forward, back into the parking space, and she sped past it.

"Fuck! They're driving off!" I yelled as I leaned forward in my seat. "Oh shit! They took her!"

"I'll follow," Blue said as she skidded around a turn at the end of the parking lot. The music that had been playing was interrupted when Blue's phone rang, and she reached out to touch the screen and answer. Before he could get a word out, she was yelling, "Someone kidnapped Sis, and we're following them!"

"What?" Bug's voice boomed out of the speakers. "Where?"

"Oh God," I whispered as I watched the car in front of us get onto the highway.

"They're on the loop headed east, just passing the Galen exit," Blue told him as she followed at a distance. "What do I do?"

"Just stay back, but don't lose them," Bug told her. "We're going to come to you. We'll cut them off at the highway."

"They're going too fast, Bug," I told him as I watched the sign for the highway exit come up ahead of us.

"Stay on them, Pickle. We'll find you," Chef's voice assured me.

"We just passed the highway. It looks like they're

getting ready to . . ."

"Oh shit!" I yelled as I saw movement in the backseat of the car. "She's fighting him in the backseat. Oh shit!"

"They're pulling over, Bug," Blue told our friend as we watched the car ahead of us screech to a halt on the side of the road. The driver's side door opened, and a man jumped out. Blue aimed the truck right for him as she slammed on her brakes. She hit him and his open door as she slid to a stop, angling her truck in front of the car.

It seemed like everything was in slow motion as I watched the man and his car door flip up over the truck. Blue and I bailed out of the truck, and I heard Bug and Chef yelling at us, asking what just happened.

The rear door on the driver side flew open, and Sis fell out onto the asphalt, dragging a man out of the car with her. I heard Blue yelling and then two gunshots before a man screamed. I was focused on the man straddling Sis and plowed into him with a running tackle just as he raised his arm to hit her.

I ended up on top of him as we fell to the gravel. He reached up and put his hands around my throat just as my first punch connected with his face. I lost track of how many times I hit him, but he never let go of my neck. I could hear Sis screaming and the roar of motorcycles, but I was focused on killing the man beneath me.

Suddenly, I saw feet step up beside us and then Blue pressed the gun into the man's forehead and said, "Let her fucking go, or I'll end you right here and fucking now."

The man's hands dropped down to the side, but I

didn't care. I kept punching him left, then right, over and over again until someone picked me up and pulled me off of him. I kicked and fought, trying to get away.

"I'm not finished," I yelled at whoever was holding me.

"Settle, Brea," I heard Santa say in my ear. "We got this. Get to Sis."

"Oh God!" I wailed as Santa put me back on my feet. I saw my daughter standing just a few feet away. She was dusty and had a few scratches, but when I pulled her into my arms, I could tell she wasn't hurt. She was fighting mad and ready to strike. "Are you okay?"

"Kill him," Sis growled.

"Okay, sweetheart. Just give us a minute," Hook told her as he pulled us into his arms. "We gotcha, girls. It's okay."

I heard a loud roar and opened my eyes. I could see Chef over Hook's shoulder. He picked up the man I'd been fighting and held him up in the air over his head before he slammed him down into the pavement. Boss and Santa jumped in front of Chef to hold him back, and he batted them to the side like they were weightless.

"You can't kill him until we talk to him," Boss yelled at Chef as he scrambled to get up off the ground. "I'll let you do it, but we need to talk to him first!"

Chef stood there with his hands fisted at his sides as he looked down at the unconscious man at his feet. We were at least 10 feet away from him, but I could hear his breathing as he tried to calm down. Finally, he leaned forward and roared so loudly that it made me and Sis jump. Chef rushed over to the two of us. He wrapped his arms around me and Sis and gently pulled us into his chest.

The man that had been in a murderous rage two seconds ago held onto us like we were delicate and breakable as he whispered, "It's okay. My girls are okay. I'm here now, Pickle. It's okay, Sis. I've got you."

Sis pulled back. It was too much, and she needed her space. Chef understood that. She stepped a few feet back from the two of us and stared up at Chef.

"Remember what you told me? Remember what you said?"

"I do, sweetheart, and I will," Chef said firmly before he nodded at my daughter. "I'm gonna make them hurt first, though."

CHEF

I watched as Frankie picked the gravel out of Hook's elbow and winced when I heard Boss cuss from just a few feet away where Jenn was working on the palm of his hand.

"I'm sorry, guys," I said honestly. "I wasn't in my right mind."

"I've got road rash on my ass, man," Santa complained from where he was laying half-naked on the table in Hook's surgery suite. A large section of his jeans and underwear had been cut away, and Blue was bent over him with a pair of tweezers picking rocks out of his thigh, hip, and ass. "You tossed me like I was a rag doll. I slid at least six feet."

"I know. I was kind of caught up in the moment." I felt horrible. Not only had I fucked the guy up that we needed to talk to, but I'd hurt three of my friends in the process.

"Fuck, man, we don't blame you," Boss told me. "Shit happens. Although, I'm gonna know better than to get in front of your big ass next time. I'll just fucking shoot you in the leg or something."

"That was some WWE shit," Preacher chimed in. "That fucker weighs at least 200 pounds, and you picked him up like he was nothing."

While I'd held onto Brea and the two of us had calmed Sis, my brothers had picked up the man in the road and tossed him into the bed of Blue's truck where the other man and the car door had landed when she hit them. Preacher and Bug had dragged the man Blue had shot out of the grass and dumped him in the back, too, before they both jumped into the bed for the ride to Hook and Paula's.

We'd dumped the men, the car, and the truck at the well house behind Boss and Jenn's before all of us had come over to Hook and Paula's so my friends could get some medical attention for the wounds I'd caused. Bug and Kitty were with them now while we waited for Sin and some of his guys to get here.

I glanced up when Brea walked into the room. She

came straight toward me and wrapped her arms around my waist.

"How's Sis?" I murmured as I held her close.

Brea shook her head in disbelief and said, "Oddly enough, she's fine. She's half asleep on the couch with Tonya, watching RuPaul critique drag routines."

"Are you okay?"

"I've never been so scared in my life," Brea admitted so softly that it was hard to hear her. "I thought I was going to lose her."

"I was terrified and too far away to help."

"Shit. These two had it handled," Hook said cheerfully.

"I do have to admit that coming up on Brea going all Tyson and Blue going Dirty Harry was pretty fucking hot," Preacher said from the stool he had placed near Santa's head. "Brea beat that guy so hard that it changed his DNA."

"Yeah, just look at him. His face looks more like a frog now than a human," Santa agreed. "She fucked him up good."

"That was some good shooting, Blue," Boss complimented her. "You hit a moving target twice. We should work on your aim, though. You didn't hit the center mass."

"I was trying to paralyze him, not kill him."

"That's why you shot him in the ass?"

"Yeah. I was going for the lower spine so his legs would drop out from under him. I missed and got him in the ass instead."

"One in each cheek," Preacher chuckled. "You're now a literal pain in his ass."

"I've got four more bullets in my gun, Preacher," Blue threatened.

The guys all laughed, but I could tell Blue was on edge. She was a convicted felon in possession of a firearm. She'd hit a man with her truck and then shot another. At least all Brea had done was beat the shit out of someone, although he might have been pretty close to dead before I body slammed him into the asphalt.

Boss's phone dinged, and he picked it up and read the message before he glanced at me and Brea. "Soda's on his way over to sit with Sis. The car's been taken care of, and Blue's truck is already in the shop. He's got Fish and Chewie cleaning it up and restoring it back to new. They'll have to wait a few days for some parts and pieces, but they'll get it back as quickly as they can."

"I'm glad you drive a truck," Brea said to our friend. "Imagine if we'd been in a Prius or something."

Blue laughed and said, "We'd have probably bounced off."

"He was an awfully large guy," Santa mused. "I'd think if you were in a car, he'd have done more damage to it than it would have to him."

"What about Sis's car?"

"It's gone. My guess is that they've dropped it somewhere already thinking that Sis was out of the equation. I called Wrecker, and he's filing a report that it was stolen. When the call comes in that it's been found, he'll take care of everything. He'll just write it up as a stolen vehicle that was found, and no one will even know Sis was involved."

Brea nodded. "Is there anything I can do to help?"

"I'm done over here," Paula told us as she finished bandaging Hook's arm. "Brea, Chef, let me look at your hands."

"My hands are fine. I never hit anyone," I told Paula as I pushed Brea away from my chest and lifted her hands up. "I'm sorry, Pickle. I never even thought about your hands."

Brea shrugged and shook her head.

Paula reached up and brushed Brea's hair back over her shoulder as she looked at her neck. "You need to stop talking for a few days . . ."

"Hallelujah! My prayers have been answered!" Preacher shouted as he put his hands together as if he was praying. He stared up at the ceiling and said, "Walt Disney was right. When you wish on a star, all your dreams really do come true."

"Shut up, Preacher!" Paula, Jenn, and Blue all yelled at the same time.

I heard Brea wheezing out a laugh, and I glared at her. "Shhhh." She made the motion to zip her lips and throw away the key, but I just shook my head, knowing that wouldn't last very long.

I stared down at Brea's hands and wasn't shocked to see that all of her knuckles were swollen. There were cuts here and there, probably from the man's teeth. I could see that she'd already washed up and put some antibacterial gel on them, probably while she was inside with Sis.

"Come here, Brea," Paula said as she washed her hands at the sink. She dried them and then put on a new pair of gloves from the box on the wall. I let Brea go to her friend as I watched Blue stand up straight and rotate her neck before she bent forward and went back to work on Santa. I walked over and stood beside her before I asked, "Is there anything I can do to help?"

"Can you take me to the gym and teach me how to hold a man over my head?"

"Probably not anytime soon. You sort of have to work up to it and then lose your fucking mind and go into a murderous rage."

"You might be able to already," Preacher added as he leaned forward and used a squeeze bottle to wash away some of the rocks, dirt, and blood Blue was dealing with on Santa's thigh. "In extreme circumstances, people can lift more than they ever thought possible. There's been reports of regular, everyday women lifting a car to get to their trapped baby or picking up a piece of debris after an accident so they can get to someone they love. It's usually a kid, but I bet it just depends on the person and circumstance."

"What he's saying is you might not be able to do something like that to save Preacher, but maybe you would to save your son or one of the girls," I explained.

"I'd lift up a car to save Preacher," Blue said softly.

"Thanks, Blue," Preacher returned quietly, and I was surprised at his tone of voice and the expression of serenity on his face. "I'd pick up a car to save you too."

Santa started humming the wedding march, and Blue slapped his injured ass cheek with her gloved hand and barked, "Shut the fuck up, Christopher."

"I'm going to tell Granny that you tortured me while you were supposed to be taking care of me."

"Shut up, you whiny ass," Blue growled. "I'll tell her that you are dating a tattooed stripper named Luscious."

"How dare you! She's a nice lady!" Hook yelled before he burst into laughter.

"I'm not dating someone named Luscious!"

"She doesn't know that, and with your reputation, who's she gonna believe?"

I rolled my eyes and walked over to Brea, leaving Preacher to sort out the family argument brewing at the surgical table.

"Will you either stay here with Paula, or go over to Jenn's with her until I'm finished? It might take a while," I explained to Brea as I watched Paula examine the knuckles on her right hand.

"She's gonna stay here and lay down so I can put some ice on her throat and her hands. How are your knees, Brea?" Paula asked as she let Brea's hand go. Brea stepped back and held her leg out, and I saw that the knees of her jeans were ripped and bloody. "Well, shit. Let me go get you a pair of shorts, and we'll get to work as soon as Santa's done on the table."

"Why didn't you say anything, Pickle? That shit has to hurt," I whispered as I gently pulled her into my arms. "You ready to cry yet?"

Brea shook her head.

"You gonna wait until we're alone to do that?"

Brea nodded against my chest, and I smiled.

"I love you, Pickle."

Brea didn't say a word, but she squeezed me tighter to let me know she loved me too.

14

CHEF

"Did the guy wake up?" I asked Bug as I walked into the well house where he'd been sitting with the three men who'd kidnapped Sis.

"He did. And, oddly enough, the dead guy woke up too," Bug told me with a laugh. "He's all jacked up and in almost as much pain as you've probably planned for the others, but he's awake."

"Is that why there's tape over his mouth?"

"He was really loud," Bug said innocently. "I offered him Tylenol, but he just shook his head."

"You got three pills out of the bottle and threw them at him. After you'd taped his mouth shut," Kitty reminded Bug. "You think he can absorb the shit through his open wounds or what?"

Bug just slowly raised his shoulders in an exaggerated shrug. I stared at the two, not sure if they were joking. They definitely didn't give a shit that there were three men in pain, tied up and moaning in the corner of the room.

"Are you talking to them now, or are we waiting on the others?" Bug asked as he stood up and stretched his arms above his head.

"I got Brea settled on the couch, so I walked over

before they were ready."

"Can't let you kill them until Boss gets to ask them some questions, man," Kitty told me as he slowly shook his head.

"What I'm going to do to them is not going to be quick, brother. From the second Blue answered the phone and we found out they took Sis, to the time we pulled up and I saw my old lady beating the shit out of that guy with Sis safe a few feet away felt like it took 10 years. It was like swimming through molasses. I couldn't get to them fast enough. These guys owe me about 10 years worth of pain, according to my estimation."

"The girls took care of shit until we got there, though, didn't they?"

Bug laughed with Kitty for a second before he agreed, "Oh, hell yeah, they did."

"That Brea's a brawler, that's for damn sure," Preacher said as he walked into the room. Boss and the rest of my brothers along with a few men from the Ares Infidels MC filed in behind him. "She beat that boy like a dirty rug."

"I should have let her kill him. She damn sure wanted to and she was well on the way from what I could tell," Santa added.

"Damn," Executioner said before he let out a long whistle. "How long have you been working those three over?"

"Haven't touched them yet," Boss informed him. He pointed to each man as he described how they got their injuries, "Blue hit that one with her truck and then shot that one twice. Brea tackled this guy and then beat him until Santa pulled her off of him. He's right. She'd have killed him if she'd had a few more minutes."

Hook picked up a chair and set it down close to the men in the corner. He looked at them and said, "I honestly thought that we'd get them here and two would already be dead. Looks like Bumper Boy over here is breathing, though. I bet he wishes he wasn't."

"He's really gonna wish he wasn't in about three minutes," Boss said as he pulled on a pair of surgical gloves. "Glove up, boys. We don't want to touch these pieces of shit and accidentally get herpes or something."

"That's not really how you get herpes," Hook started to explain, and Boss gave him a bored look. Hook glanced at the bag of cleaning supplies I'd brought over from Hook's house. "Although, you're right. I have a feeling Chef's gonna get creative, and I bet it gets messy."

"Which one should we talk to first?" Captain asked as he pulled on a pair of gloves. "I think we should save the one with three assholes for last. He's probably the most cognizant, and it might make his lips a little looser if he sees what we have in store for him."

"He was the passenger. Sis said he slapped her when she wouldn't shut up. I might need to take his hand off for that," I told the men. "I think we should take care of the other one that got hit by the truck first. Then we'll get the one Brea beat the shit out of next. I have plans for that fucker. He's going to give me my 10 years."

"Ten years?" Sin asked.

"He said that's how long it felt like from the time we found out what was going on until we got there," Kitty explained.

"When your woman's in danger, that's what it seems like. Time stands still, and you can't move quickly enough," Sin agreed.

"Well, let's drag him up onto the table then. No sense in us getting a backache bending dealing with him on the floor," Boss said as he started for the men in the corner. "Crash test dummy is the first contestant."

I watched as Hook, Boss, Bug, and Kitty dragged the man Blue had hit with her truck onto the table. They were none too gentle and from the looks of the guy, I was amazed he was still conscious. I got closer to him and looked at his face. That's when I understood why he was still awake. "He's so high that I'd be surprised if he feels any pain at all."

Hook leaned over the man and nodded his head as he lifted the man's sleeves and inspected his arms. "He's got track marks. I'd guess heroin. Looks like long-term IV drug use. The gloves were a really good idea."

"What's my name?" Boss asked.

The men around us all chuckled for a second and then Sin reached out and snatched the duck tape off the man's mouth. He sucked in a big breath, and I knew he was about to scream, so I covered his mouth and nose with my hand to cut off his air supply.

"Tsk tsk, buddy," Sin said with an evil grin. "It looks

like the big guy likes to hear dirtbags whine about as much as I do."

"I'm gonna ask you a question, and you're gonna answer me without a lot of that screaming bullshit. Got me?" Boss asked the man that was turning an alarming shade of red under my hand. "Where were you supposed to take the girl?"

I leaned down and stared the man in the eyes for a second before I took my hand off his face. He gasped for air but didn't say anything. I moved my hand to put it back over his face, and he whispered, "No, no, no. I'll tell you. Anything."

"Why did you choose our girl?" Boss asked.

"Small waist. Big boobs. Young."

"Like a shopping list?"

"Yes," the man croaked out. It sounded wet. I knew he was probably bleeding internally, and we didn't have much time to get more from him. I moved my hand to hurry Boss along.

"Who do you give the girls to?"

"Blonde man. We do the drop and get cash."

"Where do you drop them?"

The man coughed and grimaced when he tried to catch his breath. He coughed again, and it ended with a gasp as his entire body seized up and then relaxed. His eyes were open, staring at the ceiling, but he wasn't breathing.

"Well, that was unfulfilling," I mumbled as I turned

and looked at the men in the corner. "Try to do better, you two."

Boss sighed and yanked the guy off the table by the front of his shirt. He tossed his body over into the corner like he was weightless, and it landed on the other two who were tied up and waiting. Both men flinched, and one of them had tears running down his face.

"You think the girls you snatched up and sold off cried like that, fucker?" Pitbull asked before he kicked the man's hip, aiming for the middle of the blood stain in the hopes he'd get the bullet wound. "Shut the waterworks down, or I'll scoop your fucking eyes out. You don't need eyes to talk, and those fucking tears are pissing me off."

"Your old lady's okay? What about your daughter?" Executioner asked as he pulled on a pair of gloves. "Are they hurt at all?"

"Brea's hands are fucked up from hitting him, and her knees are ripped up from the gravel she was kneeling in while she was on top of him, but they'll be okay. Sis was shook up, but I told her I'd take care of them, and she let it go and went to lay down on the couch."

"Good," Executioner said as he glanced over at the corner. "I'll help."

"Who's next?" Boss asked as he walked over to stand next to Pitbull. "The one with two new assholes is bleeding like a stuck pig and he finally quit crying."

"Bring him over," I said as I watched Pitbull drag the man by one foot across the room before he lifted him up by the shirt until he was sitting on the edge of the table. He then slammed him down onto his back and actually growled at him before he moved back so Boss and Sin could talk to the guy.

The two men questioned him for at least 30 minutes, gathering every detail they could from him before they decided he'd served his purpose.

"Chef, what are you cooking over there?" Boss called out when he realized I was at the bar mixing something together in a bowl.

"Soup's almost done, Boss. Can you give our guest some water? A good amount. All that crying probably dehydrated him."

Boss raised one eyebrow but shrugged and motioned for Kitty to hand him the half-empty bottle of water he held in his hand. Once he had it, he made the man drink the rest of the bottle before he tossed it in the trash can against the wall.

"Three points!" Boss cheered.

"That was not a three-point shot," Sin argued. "You're way too close for that. That was barely a fucking free throw."

"Do you need glasses?"

"I think you need glasses, old man. Your depth perception is off," Sin scoffed. "I set myself up for that, but if a goddamn one of you says anything about my dick, I will end you."

"You threw that door open knowing what we'd be

thinking, Sin," Santa teased. "We all get points for resisting."

Kitty leaned his head back and blew out a breath before he whined, "It's so hard."

"That's what she said!" at least three men crowed before the room erupted in laughter.

"Soup's done," I announced as I picked up the bowl containing the mixture I'd made. "You guys might want to step back."

The men took me at my word and stepped away from the table, all of them up against the walls now, as far away as they could get without outright leaving the room.

"This is some of that chef shit you got your name for, isn't it?" Executioner asked as he warily eyed the bowl I was carrying. "Do we need gas masks or something?"

"Nope. This doesn't have toxic fumes. The chemical reaction doesn't occur until it comes into contact with something like water, blood, or sweat. Three things that this man has in abundance right now."

"Okay," Executioner mumbled, not quite convinced.

"Trust me. I went to college for this shit and then earned my doctorate while I was in prison."

"Yeah," Phantom scoffed. "We saw what Boss learned in prison, and that still grosses me the fuck out."

"You might wanna go outside for a few minutes then," I warned him before I looked down at the man tied up on the table in front of me. "You took our girl and put her life in danger. It felt like lava in my chest, burning its way through my body when I heard her mama screaming in fear for her baby girl. I want you to know what that feels like, but since I'm not the kind to go and kidnap innocent girls who are just out minding their own fucking business, your family is safe. You, however, are not. I'll see you in hell, fucker. Your trip getting there is gonna hurt like a bitch."

The man opened his mouth to argue, and I used my free hand to grip his lower jaw, pushing my thumb and forefinger in on either side of his face, squeezing his cheeks in so he couldn't close his mouth. I tipped the bowl up and poured the mixture into his mouth before I slammed his mouth closed and held it there.

The chemical reaction was instantaneous. Since he couldn't spit it out, he had no other option but to swallow. I could hear the chemicals fizzing as they worked their way down his esophagus to the water he'd just gulped down not five minutes ago.

"The more water, the more reaction. Right now, you're burning from the inside out, and that's not even a fraction of the pain I felt when I thought of our girl, terrified and fucking stuck in a car with you," I hissed as I stared down into his pain-filled eyes.

"Fuck. Did he just pour Drano down his throat?" I heard Pitbull whisper. "That's twisted as hell."

"No shit." Executioner chuckled. "An eye for an eye. Well, in this case, a hole in your gut for a hole in your gut, I guess."

"Is he dead?" Boss asked just as the man started to convulse. "Guess not. Let's move him closer to the floor drain, why don't we?"

"Good plan," Santa agreed as he grabbed the man by his boot and tugged him toward the end of the metal table. "He's not going to explode when he hits the ground, is he?"

I tilted my head and pursed my lips as I studied the man. "It's the first time I've ever done that, so I'm not really sure."

"So fucked up," Executioner whispered. "Does *anyone* get rehabilitated in prison?"

"I haven't robbed anyone since before I went in," Santa professed. "Neither has Kitty."

"The only fires I've started have been in the fire pit at our house. I swear. I'm a changed man. See? The system works!"

Executioner, Pitbull, Sin, and Phantom stared at Bug like he'd just sprouted horns. My friend didn't see the irony in the fact that he'd gone to prison as an arsonist and was now a criminal accessory to three counts of first-degree murder along with at least 20 other charges we'd racked up tonight. But, by God, he hadn't burned any buildings down, had he?

Santa gave one final yank, and the man's body made a loud thump when it hit the floor. I saw Kitty and Bug flinch as if they were afraid he'd explode on impact. There was a collective sigh of relief when nothing happened.

"I kind of wish he'd popped," Santa said under his breath as he dragged the man closer to the drain. "That wasn't rewarding at all."

Boss and Hook laughed, and I saw Preacher shaking his head with a smile.

"Who do we have next, Bob?" Captain asked cheerfully as he walked over to the last man in the corner. "Well, Johnny, it looks like we're down to the final contestant. The first one couldn't give us much, the second one got choked up in the end, but we've got high hopes for number three!"

"What did I miss?" Stamp asked breathlessly as he slid into the room like Kramer from that old television show. "Shit. I missed two of them? Fuck!"

"Where have you been?"

"I was in Albuquerque then Clayton, and today, I was in Rojo," Stamp explained as he pulled on a pair of gloves. "I had some great food while I was out of town, though. I filmed at this diner in Rojo today. The best meatloaf I've ever fucking tasted, man. The chocolate pie was to die for. It's worth the drive just for the food."

"Hmm. If it's that good, we might just have to take a road trip. We've got some friends who own a custom build shop in Rojo. We ship them parts, on occasion. Maybe we'll go in the fall when it's a little cooler outside." Boss suggested. "Sin, we should plan that for both clubs. It sounds fun. Maybe make a weekend of it and take the ladies with us."

"That sounds good," I agreed. "By then, Sis will have her bike built and should have plenty of experience on it, so she'll be ready for a long ride."

"Today, people! Let's get this show on the road. I've been binge watching Criminal Minds, and I want to get a few episodes in before bed. I have court early tomorrow morning, and I can't be late," Captain explained as he dragged the man who was kicking and fighting across the floor toward the table. "A little help here?"

"Oh shit," Pitbull said as he rushed over to help. "Which season are you on?"

"Eight, I think," Captain answered after a few seconds of contemplation.

"Is Prentiss on there?" Preacher asked. "She came back in season six or seven."

"Yeah, Prentiss came back, but she's gone again. There's a new girl. The brunette from the polygamy show."

Preacher thought for a second and then asked, "Big Love?"

"Yeah. The main wife."

"Oh, you're in eight then," Pitbull told him as they settled the man on the table and held him down while they talked. "Her voice is sexy as hell. The way she talks is *very* hot teacher."

"You know who I think is hot? Garcia. Damn. That woman."

"I'd have to agree, Preach," I told him. "Baby Girl is the shit."

"Have you noticed that they get easily distracted?" Boss asked Sin. "They're like puppies."

"Or squirrels," Sin mused. "Look! Shiny!"

Pitbull flipped the two men off as he walked back over and sat on one of the barstools.

It took a while, but the last man, the one that had held Sis in the backseat and then choked Brea on the side of the road, answered every question they had as he laid there quivering with fear.

"What's the recipe for this one?" Sin asked, taking off his gloves as he walked past me toward the refrigerator to get a beer. "Anyone else want a cold one?"

"I'll take one," I told him. "This could take a while, and I'm parched."

"What are you going to do?" Boss asked me.

"I'm going to show him what it's like to have an elephant sitting on your chest while you're so fucking scared that you feel like your heart's about to explode, and you can't catch your breath."

"How are you going to do that?"

"Today, I'm an elephant," I told Boss as I climbed up on the table and straddled the man's chest. As I slowly let my weight settle on him, I stared down into his eyes. "I'm not gonna beat you. My woman did that. I'm going to demonstrate to you how I felt knowing they were in danger and not being able to protect them. I'll do it until you're dead. I'm going to slowly suffocate you until either your ribs crack and puncture your lungs or your heart explodes because it has to work double time to beat. Right when it seems like it's your last breath, I'm going to sit up and let you take one in, then I'm going to start all over again, bringing you to the brink over and over."

"Totally fucked up," Executioner grumbled. "But that's so fucking creative."

15

BREA

"I'm not here to pick at you," Preacher said the second I opened my front door. "Okay, I'm gonna try really hard not to pick at you. Let's put it that way."

I stared at him for a minute before I stepped back and let him into the house. Chef and Sis had left less than an hour ago to run to the store for the stuff we didn't get last night. She was obsessing about building the bird a play gym, and that was okay. It would take her mind off of everything and let her process things at her own pace.

I, on the other hand, had barely slept last night. The man I'd beaten on the side of the road had somehow found my biggest weakness. My trigger, so to speak.

He'd wrapped his hands around my throat, just like it happened every night in my dreams, and now, I was a walking zombie because every time I closed my eyes, I relived it all. The few times I had fallen asleep, my nightmare had started, and I was awake within an hour or so. Chef had been right there with me, waking up every time and trying his hardest to relax me back into slumber. He'd tried sex, cup of hot tea, more sex, a back massage, and more sex. Not that I was complaining, mind you. All of those things were awesome, and the fact that he felt the need to take care of me brought tears to my eyes.

But right now, he had to be as exhausted or even more

so than I was.

"I brought you something. As much as I can't stand you yammering at me, I know your head will probably explode if you can't get the words out," Preacher explained as he opened his backpack and pulled out a bag from a store in town. He dug through it and then handed me a small dry erase board and a pack of markers to go with it. I stood there in shock, staring at the gift in my hands.

Preacher and I didn't hate each other, by any means. Somehow, we just rubbed each other the wrong way. I loved the man because he was a loyal friend to my daughter and treated her like she was his sweet little sister. I knew that he would do anything in the world for her. I also knew that as much as he grumbled about me, he'd do anything for me too.

Tears welled up in my eyes, but Preacher didn't notice. He was pulling things out of the bag and stacking them on the board in my hands.

"Here's a box of Kleenex to wipe the marker off, so you don't have to use your fingers. I also got a bottle of this special cleaner for the board. I opened it, and I'm pretty sure it's just rubbing alcohol, but . . ."

I dropped the stuff he'd been stacking in my hands and wrapped my arms around my friend and hugged him tight. He let out an 'oof' when I hit his chest, but in the next second, his hands were on my back, and he was holding me tight as I sobbed into his shirt.

"Oh shit," Preacher whispered as he rubbed his hands up and down my back. "It's okay. Sis is okay, it's all gonna be okay. You're safe and Sis is safe, honey. We'll take care of you. You know we will."

I started to say something, and Preacher somehow knew. He squeezed me just a little tighter, and I nodded.

"Dammit, woman," Preacher grumbled as he moved us toward the couch. "Come sit with me for a minute, and get this shit out. My mama said that tears were the poison coming out, you know? She said that if you kept them in there, they'd rot you from the inside out. You just do your thing, and I'm gonna let you as long as you don't get snot on my shirt."

Through my tears, I had to laugh. I was sitting next to him, resting my head on his chest as I listened to my old friend talk about his mom, his grandma, and random other things while he tried to comfort me.

I was so warm and relaxed that I finally just let go and closed my eyes.

"Shit! Wake up, woman!" I heard Preacher bark, and it shocked me out of my nightmare. "What the fuck is wrong?"

I was next to him on the couch, gasping for air and clutching at the bruises on my throat, while I tried to shake off the nightmare.

My usual dream had morphed into a mixture of the night I killed a woman and last night, when the man had his hands around my neck. Somehow, the two had intertwined, and I'd been back in that shitty house on the floor of the kitchen, but his hands were around my neck, not hers.

"Fuck. Are you okay? What the hell was that about?" Preacher asked before he put his hand up and shook his head. He jumped up off the couch and went over to the pile of things I'd dropped. He picked them all up and brought them over to the couch. He dropped everything onto the coffee table, ripped open the package of markers, and handed me one along with the dry erase board. He opened the box of tissues and pulled one out before he dabbed my face. "You write down what that dream was about, Brea. Was it about what happened last night?"

I shook my head and hesitated before I shrugged and nodded.

"Your dreams are stuck on repeat, huh? Are they mixing up? Write it down, and we'll talk about it." I shook my head, and he tapped his fingers on the board and then stared at me for a second before he said, "They're the same as your tears, babe. Don't let them fester inside you."

I picked the board up and wrote, '*Night I got arrested. Killed a woman.*'

"You went in for murder? Manslaughter?"

'*She was hurting her little boy. I stopped her. We fought. She choked me, but I beat her to death.*'

"Shit. Okay. And you dreamed about that because the fucker choked you last night, huh?"

'*Dream almost every night.*'

"You're not okay that she died? She was hurting a kid,

the bitch deserved it."

'In my dreams, she kills us both.'

"What happened to the kid? I'm sure he's out there somewhere living his life, honey. You've just got it all twisted in your mind. You need to talk to the kid. Is he related to you? How did you know him?"

'My dealer's girlfriend's son. He went to prison for the drugs. I went back for a violation - not killing her. Boy was put in foster care, I guess. Don't know where he is or if he's okay.'

"That's why you're dreaming. You don't have any closure. You tried to protect him and can't be sure he's okay. I'm sure they put you in the back of a car, and that was it. No more information, huh?"

I shook my head as I cleaned off the board with a tissue.

"Now, years later, you're all fucked up. How long has it been?"

I held one hand up to show him five, then closed and opened my hand twice to tell him it had been 15 years.

"How big was the kid? Baby? Talking? In school?"

I shrugged and put my hand up at about the height I thought the boy would be and wrote, *'Tall but too skinny. Not healthy. No idea.'*

"Hmm. It was the town you came from, right? Fifteen years ago. Kid would be 20 to 25 years old now, I guess."

I nodded.

"It's got you all fucked up, Brea." I shrugged and leaned back against the couch cushions. "Have you ever tried sleeping pills?"

I shook my head and wrote, '*Take pills then can't wake up. Nightmare goes on and on, and I can't get out.*'

"I can see that might happen. Okay, listen. I'm gonna sit here and do some research for a release I've got coming up. You're gonna get that pillow over there and lay down right here beside me and fucking go to sleep. If you start twitching like you did before, I'll wake you up. I promise. Then when you calm down, you go to sleep again. I've got all day. We'll get you some rest, even if it is in spurts."

I shook my head.

"One good thing about those bruises on your neck is that, for once, you can't argue with me. Now, lay your ass down right here on the couch, let me play with your hair or some shit to get you relaxed, and you're gonna sleep while I work."

I was so damn tired and sore. Sleep sounded wonderful, so I didn't even try to argue. I reached for the pillow at the other end of the couch and then settled my head next to Preacher's hip and closed my eyes. I felt him get up and move around the living room. I got choked up when I felt him lay an afghan over me and tuck it around my feet and legs before he sat back down.

I relaxed as Preacher started humming to the song playing softly through my stereo. I was surprised that he knew the tune. Andra Day's "Rise Up" was one of my favorite songs. Preacher's deep voice came out and perfectly harmonized with the singer as he went back and forth between playing with my hair and rubbing my back.

I was so comfortable under the soft blanket, and I felt safe and secure next to my old friend. I was thinking about how lucky I was to have people like Preacher around me when sleep took me under.

CHEF

I flipped my phone open and read the text from Preacher. He was at our house with Brea, and she was sleeping on the couch. He wanted to warn me to be quiet when I came in so I didn't wake her.

I couldn't imagine how that visit had gone with Brea not being able to argue with Preacher. The two of them fought like brother and sister, and it had to be absolutely killing her to not be able to say anything. They seemed to enjoy giving each other shit, but I was glad she was comfortable and relaxed enough to get a nap in with him there.

"What else are you thinking, Sis?"

"I researched it, and we need different sizes so he doesn't get cramps in his feet."

I was standing in the plumbing aisle of the hardware store with a basket of shit Sis and I were going to put together like Tinker Toys for a bird. A bird who had just this morning, not only insulted me, but my mom, too, when I walked over to get Sis.

The little bastard needed to be cooking in a pot with some dumplings, but she wanted to build it a fucking jungle gym. I just didn't understand these women and their animals, and I probably never would.

I was living in a house with three small dogs who thought the world revolved around them, and from the way Brea and Sis acted, the world really did. I lost my fucking keys this morning and had to search for them for 15 minutes before I found them in the box Brea had built to house the fucking rodents. The damn hedgehog stole them to take back to his nest and give to the love of his life, a fucking possum of all things. While I was in there, I found a stash of earrings, a bunch of change, a refrigerator magnet, and a variety of bolts and screws that were a complete mystery to Brea.

We were going to set something down somewhere one day, and the furniture was going to collapse because that little fucker was steadily dismantling it.

This was my life now, but I loved every second of it.

I needed to get a big dog of my own to balance shit out. Or maybe I could just take Tonya from Hook. That might work.

"Earth to Chef," Sis said as she snapped her fingers in front of my face.

I reached up and moved her arm down as I asked, "What did I miss?"

"Can we make the perches different sizes?"

"Yeah. Let me show you the finer points of PVC connections, sweetheart. You can go apeshit finding all the parts and pieces you think we'll need, but I imagine we'll end up back here at least five times. That's just how it works."

"You're very good to me, Chef."

I was stunned. Sis didn't often talk about her emotions, and she wasn't one to just drop compliments. I said the first thing that came to mind and watched her face light up. "Because I love you, Sis."

"Of course you do. I'm very lovable."

"Yeah. You are," I told her as I stopped in front of the shelf that contained all the boxes of PVC connectors. "Now, go nuts, Sis. Shop to your heart's content. I finally found something I can buy a woman that won't cost an arm and a leg."

Sis looked at the cart I was pushing and then up at me with one eyebrow raised before she asked, "Is that a challenge?"

———————⬡———————

I pulled my boots off on the back porch and carried them in my hands as I walked into the house. I didn't want to make any noise that might wake Brea if she was still asleep. When I walked into the living room, I found Brea curled up under an afghan, and Preacher sitting next to her working on his laptop.

The thieving hedgehog and the damn possum were snuggled up on top of Brea's hip. One of the dogs was curled up in her arms with his head poking out from under the blanket while another was resting on her feet. The little brown fur ball that liked to destroy shoes was asleep on the back of the couch behind Preacher. Before he realized I was there, I saw him reach up and rub the little guy between his ears.

Jesus. They'd converted Preacher too. What was the world coming to?

"Hey," I whispered from the doorway. Preacher slowly turned to look at me. "How's she doing?"

"She's up and down. Sleeps like the dead and then wakes up gasping for air. It's happened twice in the last hour." I shook my head, wondering how to help Brea. This couldn't be good for her health, going without good rest for weeks on end, but I didn't know how to fix it. "I know shit's still going down, but I've talked to Boss about taking a short road trip. Are you up for it? We'd be gone for a day, maybe overnight."

"I hate to leave Brea and Sis right now, brother."

"I get that, but this is for them. Well, for Brea at least. I'd like for you to come. Maybe Santa too. He can be charming and people just like both of you almost instantly, for some reason."

"It's my good looks and charming personality."

Preacher just stared at me flatly. "I think Blue should come with us. She can ride with either me or Santa. We need a girl to round out the group."

"What are we doing?"

"We're going hunting, and we're going to bring back

a solution to Brea's sleep problems, my friend."

16

CHEF

"How are Brea and Sis?" Hook asked as I adjusted the weights on the machine I was using for squats.

"Brea's not sleeping for shit. Sis seems to be okay, but she's jumpy and won't drive anywhere alone."

"They found her car?"

"Yeah. It was parked at the mall by the food court entrance. Just sitting there, but this time the doors were shut. I guess they knew the others had been caught, so they tried to do something different," I told him. "Brea told me to sell the fucking thing and find her a new one."

"Need help choosing one? Car or truck?"

"Well, we're taking this opportunity to check out that sleazy car dealer that Brea sees when she's at the coffee truck."

"That sounds reasonable."

"I'm not happy about giving some shady fucker my money, but a car salesman is a car salesman, I guess."

"What's the difference between a used car salesman and a catfish?"

"I'm almost afraid to ask."

"One's a scum sucking bottom dweller, and the other one's a fish."

I laughed for a second and then told him, "You need to change that car dealer to lawyer and tell it to Cap."

"I like my teeth, thank you. Preach told me you guys are taking a trip?"

"Yeah. He's got something in his head and won't tell me about it. Just expects me to hop on my bike and fucking go."

"He's gotta have a good reason if he insists on you. Santa was going to go, but he asked me to take his place this morning. Preacher told him it had something to do with Brea, and he wants to go, but he's gotta go to California for some shit."

"Paula okay with you leaving her?"

"Shit. She's probably gonna be more than okay with it. She'll have the crazy coven of girls over, and they'll probably drink too much, talk shit on all of us, feed Tonya junk food, and pass out on my furniture."

"I need a big dog."

"What?"

"I'm surrounded by weirdness, man. There's the two little French ones, one of which is a pothead when he's not running laps around the goddamn coffee table. There's the little Barbie toy you brought Sis a while back, then we've got the fucking rodents who steal all things shiny and hide inside shit. I put my fucking boot on yesterday morning and thought I killed the hedgehog. Scared the fuck out of me. How would I explain that?"

"And your answer to all those miniature animals is to bring in a big dog? You want him to *eat* the smaller animals or . . ."

"Can I borrow Tonya?"

"Hell no," Hook snapped.

"I don't want it to eat them, I just think they need an alpha. Other than me. Brea's dog Danee follows me around like I'm her intended. It's cute but strange, and I think it hurts Brea's feelings. My foot's bigger than most of the animals in my house. I need something sturdy."

"If we went back in time, let's say a year or so, would you believe we'd ever be having this conversation?"

"Did you think you'd be shacked up with a pocket-sized badass who probably has a book of ideas on how to kill people? I mean, I love your girl and all, but she's a little . . . um . . ." I paused because Hook was glaring at me. "Inventive?"

"Good save."

"Who is the cop talking to?"

Hook whispered, "That's the fucking car guy, and he looks *pissed*."

"I'm gonna go to the bathroom and see what I can pick up as I amble by," I told Hook as I leaned down and untied my shoelace. "'I'll be back shortly."

I walked across the gym at a regular pace, slowing when I got closer to the two people talking next to one of the elliptical machines. When I got within earshot, I knelt down on one knee and fiddled with my shoelace. I took my time going from one foot to the other, paying close attention to what the two of them were talking about for as long as I could until I had no choice but to stand up and walk past them on my way to the bathroom.

While I was there, I went ahead and used the facilities and washed my hands before I walked back out to Hook.

"What did they say?"

I picked up my phone and found the voice recorder app so I only had to spit out the information once while it was fresh in my mind.

He said, 'You're gonna figure out where they took that fucking car and get me the information before they delve any deeper.'

She told him, 'Impound has nothing to do with my job duties, and it would be suspicious if I got involved.'

He said, "Figure out a way, or we're all going down.'

She told him, 'That car has nothing to do with me.'

He told her, 'If you don't figure this shit out, you won't have to worry about it. You won't have to worry about anything anymore.'

She said, 'Is that a threat? You're threatening me?'

He didn't say anything, and they were quiet for a second before she said, 'I've got a guy in patrol named Harrison who owes me for keeping his little brother out of trouble. I'll get him to look into it and call you tomorrow.'

He told her, 'Don't call me. Meet me at my office at ten. Say your goodbyes first just in case I don't like what I hear.'"

"Well," Hook drawled while I saved the recording and closed out the app. "That was informative. Sort of."

"I guess we should call Boss and see if he wants to grab a cup of coffee."

"I'll text him while you lift. He's gonna want Wrecker to be there, for sure. Maybe Sin too."

"Hey, Pickle," I said with a smile as I walked up to Jenn's coffee truck. She and Brea were inside working, and Kitty was off to the side serving as their security.

"What are you doing here? I thought you were going to work out with Hook."

"I did. I'm meeting Boss and some of the guys here to talk."

"I'll get your favorite," Brea said as she leaned over the counter and gave me a quick kiss. I watched her as she worked and saw that she had dark circles under her eyes and looked utterly exhausted. I hoped that whatever Preacher had planned worked. I had a good idea, but we'd see. He insisted that we needed to leave early tomorrow morning, and we'd probably be staying the night. When I'd discussed it with Brea, she was fine with the idea and even joked that it might be the only way I'd get a good night's sleep. She turned around and winked at me as she slid my favorite coffee across the counter. "I'll expect payment for this later, big guy."

Kitty was off to the side where I couldn't see him but heard him making kissing noises, so I reached in through the window and flipped him off. He laughed for a second, and Brea just rolled her eyes.

"How does your throat feel?"

"It's okay. If I talk too long at once, it gets scratchy, but otherwise, I'm okay."

"It's only been a few days, Pickle. Maybe you should . . ."

"Maybe I'm just fine, Chef."

"Maybe you're feeling a little sassy, and we should read a book together," I told her with a salacious grin.

"Wait until my throat's all healed up, and maybe I'll read a book to you."

"You'd have to reinforce that headboard first, sweetheart," I told her with a laugh as I put my arm up and flexed.

Jenn walked back into the trailer, and I knew that likely meant Boss was ready to talk. I blew Brea a kiss and walked around the trailer.

"So, we're all here. What's up?" Boss asked after I settled my snack on the tailgate of Jenn's truck. Hook and I told him about what we'd seen, and I played the voice recording I'd made.

Boss, Wrecker, and Sin all stood there silently for a minute or two, processing what they'd heard. Finally, the three of them started talking, throwing out ideas that probably wouldn't pertain to me in the long run. I looked around the park while I listened, and across the way, I saw the slimeball car guy.

"Shit. He's here. I'm making myself disappear, guys. Call me with specifics to look for when I go car shopping in a bit," I said as I walked over and stood behind the food truck. I waited until I heard the man talking to Brea and Jenn before I walked toward my motorcycle. Hook wasn't far behind me and within just a few minutes, we were on our bikes and headed to get Sis so we could go car shopping.

"Why don't we just finish my motorcycle, and I'll ride it every day?"

"About done with this car shopping bullshit, huh?" Hook asked Sis as we walked around yet another car on the huge lot.

"Okay. I should have started it out like this. Do you want a car or truck?" I asked her.

"A truck. A normal-sized one, not one like yours."

"What color?"

"Black." I slowly nodded and looked toward the *other* end of the car lot. All of the trucks were in that direction, and we'd have to navigate a minefield of car salesmen on the way.

"Or one of those new gray ones. I like silver too."

"Hello, gentlemen," I heard a man's voice say from a few car lengths down. I closed my eyes and took a deep breath, wondering if I'd get to growl at this one or if Hook would take his turn. When I opened my eyes, I saw Hook shaking hands with that son of a bitch we'd seen at the gym and then at the park an hour or so ago. "I'm Cyrus Fairchild."

"You're the man from television." Sis looked down at his outstretched hand for a second before she finally put hers out to shake it. She subtly wiped her hand on her jeans the second he let it go.

"I am, sweetheart. Are you here with your dad for a new vehicle today?"

I watched a wicked grin cross her face before she said, "I'm here with my dads. They're helping me decide."

"You little shit," I heard Hook whisper.

"Well, it's good that you're looking into this as a family. It's a big decision." The man's words didn't match the look on his face at all, but I'd give him credit for trying. Money could motivate someone to do all sorts of things they weren't comfortable with. Just to be a dick, I decided to see how far I could push him. "Have you thought about our leasing program?"

"What's that about?" Sis asked.

"Haven't you heard of something like that, sugar?" I asked as I leaned around Sis and grinned at Hook.

Hook grumbled before he said, "I'm familiar with it,

but let's get some details, *honey*."

Sis was giggling outright now, and it was killing me to keep a straight face. Hook wasn't homophobic by any means, but he wasn't a fan of me calling him sugar, that was for damn sure.

"Well, what did you think of Sis's new ride?" I asked Brea as I watched her wash her face as we got ready for bed.

"Did she have to lease it? Why couldn't she just buy it outright?"

"Considering she won't really put a lot of miles on it, I think it's a good plan for her. She'll have plenty of support from the dealer, and in a few years, if she wants to trade up, she can do that rather than worrying about selling what she's got and dealing with the whole thing again."

"I guess. Lot's of people do that, I'm just not sure it's for me. She's happy, though, so I'm happy."

"As long as you're happy, then I've done something right, Pickle."

"I hear she shoved you and Hook out of the closet," Brea said with a grin before she bent to rinse her face. "I bet that was an adventure."

I chuckled for a second before I told her how much fun Hook and I had while we were car shopping. By the time we'd left the dealership, Sis regretted her little prank. We'd embarrassed the hell out of her with our affectionate nicknames and the fact that Hook made her start calling him Father Dear.

"Your daughter has a warped sense of humor, but we turned the tables on her, so it worked out alright."

"She told me that the two of you explained your 'sex cave' to the car guy. Was that really necessary?"

"It was highly uncomfortable for both of them, so I'd have to say yes. However, everything I was describing is what I want *our* sex cave to look like."

"We're getting a sex cave? Do tell."

"I'm thinking soundproof walls, places to tie you up, a spanking bench, a swing, and some of those angled pillows so we can try out some fun positions."

Brea's eyebrows raised but she looked thoughtful before she said, "I've got this angled pillow I got to prop up my leg when I hurt my knee last year. I wonder if that would work."

"Where is it?"

"It's in a trash bag in the attic."

"Specifically *where* in the attic?" I asked her as I slipped on my running shoes.

"On the top shelf against the north wall."

"I'll be right back."

17

BREA

"How are things going now that Chef has moved in? Is the honeymoon period still going strong or have you started plotting his death over the small things yet?" Paula asked as she took one of the drawers out of my dresser and set it on the end of my bed. Jenn pulled the next one out and set it on top of the one Paula put down. I moved around them as I carried the ladder over into the corner.

"Obviously, they're good, considering what we're about to do," Frankie laughed from the bed.

"That doesn't mean she's not thinking about it," Jenn told Frankie. "I love Boss, but there are times that he tries to strong arm me into doing something I don't want to do, and I think about poisoning his coffee."

"Aqua Tofana," Paula and I whispered in unison. Jenn and Frankie silently stared at the two of us with their brows raised. Paula broke the silence and said, "Let me send you a link to one of our favorite vloggers, and you'll understand."

"A favorite other than Blue, of course," I added. "Anyway, what does Boss do that pisses you off? What's he pushy about?"

"He harps on me about wearing my wrist braces at night. The one time I just ignored him and went to sleep, I woke to him trying to get the fucking things on me without waking me up."

"That's not pushy. That just makes sense. He's trying to take care of you. If you're too stupid to do what the doctor tells you, at least he's there to follow directions," Frankie argued. "It's not rocket science. If the doctor said to do it, then do it."

"Go get me a bottle of water," Paula ordered Frankie. When Frankie looked at her, Paula's eyes got wide and she said, "What? You said to do what the doctor told you. Go get me a fucking water."

"You're such a pain in my ass," Frankie grumbled as she got off the bed. "I don't even like you half the time."

Once Frankie was out of the room, Paula chuckled and said, "But she's getting me a fucking water, isn't she?"

"Two words: aqua tofana. Seriously," I told Paula. Paula's face fell, and she glanced at the bedroom door before she rushed out to follow Frankie into the kitchen.

"What is that about?" Jenn asked as she grabbed the edge of the dresser and leaned back to pull it toward her.

"*Do not* pull that by yourself!" I snapped at her. I walked over and batted my hands at her until she moved away. "We just talked about you needing wrist braces, and now, you're just being a dumbass."

"I don't know why I think the three of you are my friends with all your shit talking," Jenn grumbled as she sat down in the spot Frankie had just vacated.

"Because we love you and want to take care of you.

That and we're pushy bitches just like you. It's either we become friends or start trying to whip each other's ass every time we see each other, scrambling for the top position as Queen Badass."

"That's a prison reference, huh?"

"Maybe," I scoffed.

"Was there a badass no one fucked with?" Frankie asked as she joined Jenn on the bed.

Paula and I grunted and groaned as we scooted the dresser closer to the door before we started reloading the drawers.

"There's always a few," I told the girls.

"Some big woman named Bertha who has a chin mole with hair sprouting out of it?" Paula asked.

"There's always a Bertha and a Peaches every single place you go. Bertha's usually the type that insists you give her your soup."

"And do you give her your soup?" Jenn asked.

"It's either give her your soup or give her your ass, and you'll be asking that bitch what flavor noodles she wants if you know what's good for you," I told them with a laugh. "However, you've gotta be scrappy and not afraid to fight, soup or not."

"I couldn't survive in prison," Frankie admitted.

"I think I'd do okay," Paula told us. "People underestimate the short ones, but we're more evil since we're closer to hell."

All four of us laughed while Paula and I finished with the drawers. I walked over and stared up at the ceiling for a second before I blew out a breath. "Well, if I fuck it up, it's just a house, right?"

"Why are we doing this alone again? We do have men around, you know? A whole lot of them, and there's an entire company full of construction workers that could have this shit done in seconds," Jenn reminded me. "They've done all sorts of work at my house, and they're as nice as can be."

"Boss lives in your house, and he'd kill any one of them that disrespected you," Frankie reminded her.

"Well, they were nice even before I got Boss, so there," Jenn said snottily before she stuck her tongue out at Frankie.

"Wow. You're just terrifying," Paula said drolly. "Okay. It's your house, so you get to be the one that fucks with the shit in the attic. If one of us saws through something important and your fucking ceiling falls in, there will be a lot of explaining to do. If you do it, it's your own damn fault."

"So much support coming from the peanut gallery," I grumbled before I let out a sigh. "I watched a YouTube video on how to do this, and I think I've got it. If not, I'll end up in traction."

"If you do, we'll give you all our jello at lunchtime," Jenn joked. "We'll even give you our soup."

"Save the soup for Blue. She doesn't have a hairy mole on her chin, but she was Bertha on occasion. Don't let her try and convince you otherwise. However, if it's red jello, I'm all

228

about it."

CHEF

"What's the plan?" I asked Preacher as we got off our motorcycles in front of the hotel where he'd reserved our rooms. "Now that we're here, are you going to tell us why we're here?"

"Yeah, we're going on faith here, brother. Although that was a nice ride down from Tenillo. Weather was perfect," Hook said as he lifted his arms above his head and stretched.

"Blue has an appointment, and I'm taking her to it. You guys stay at the hotel, or go grab a beer somewhere. We'll call you when we need you."

"We came down for you to go to an appointment?" I asked Blue.

She grinned and put her tattoo-covered arm out before she said, "I've got a spot right here that needs some color."

"We came here for you to get a fucking tattoo? Are you kidding me?"

"We came here to make sure I'm right about something. When we confirm that I am, we'll call you and let you know where we are so you can join us."

"He's lost his fucking mind," Hook said as we walked

into the hotel to check in. "Seriously lost his fucking mind."

Once we had the room keys, we got into the elevator to go upstairs.

"Who's sharing a room with me?" I asked.

"I'm not sharing a room with you or Hook," Blue told us firmly. "Just like when we were talking about who I'd ride with. The two of you have women, and I like those girls. I'm not stepping on any toes. I'll bunk with Preacher."

"Makes sense," Hook agreed. "It's also awfully considerate of you."

"I can be considerate."

"You almost slapped the shit out of that woman when we stopped for gas on the way here," I reminded her.

"That wasn't being inconsiderate, Blue was just prickly. She looked at all of us like we were about to steal her soul or something," Preacher reminded us. "She wouldn't even walk through the door you were holding open for her."

"That could be because I'm black. It might not have anything to do with the rest of you.

"Well then, all the more reason for me to be prickly." Blue huffed out a breath and then mumbled, "Uptight, snobby, racist bitch."

"You're so cute when you're riled," Hook teased. Blue flipped him off, and Hook laughed loudly, his voice echoing down the hall as we walked to our room. He put the keycard in and we said our goodbyes to Preacher and Blue before we walked inside. Hook went to the bathroom, and I immediately headed to turn the AC down to morgue level so the room would be cool enough to sleep in tonight.

I pulled my phone out and called Brea.

"You've reached 1-900-SPANK-ME. Do you want a paddle or my bare hand?" I heard Frankie say. I pulled the phone away from my face and looked at it to make sure I'd called the right number before I pushed the speaker button and laid it down on the bed.

"How about neither?"

"What'cha doin, Chef?"

"I'm calling to talk to Brea. What are you doing?"

"I'm answering Brea's phone because she's indisposed at the moment."

"Indisposed?"

"A little bit," Frankie said before she burst into loud laughter. I heard her snort and then laugh even harder. In the background, I could hear Brea yelling, 'Pull it down, or you're going to pop my fucking leg off!' "Can I have Brea call you back in a minute?"

"What are they doing?"

"Buddy," Frankie said before she started laughing again. "I'm videoing all of it. You can see it when you get back."

"Okay. Tell Brea we made it safely, and we're going to go run around for a bit. If she calls and I don't answer, it's because I'm on the bike."

"Will do," Frankie told me. I heard Paula and Jenn cackling in the background and then Brea yelling, 'I hate both of you!'. "Bye, Chef. I'll tell. . . oh shit. Gotta go!"

"What the hell was that about?" Hook asked as he walked out of the bathroom.

"I have no idea, but the thought of those four all together and laughing that hard can't be a good thing."

"It's scary," Hook admitted. "Want to go grab something to eat and have a beer?"

"I have something different in mind. You know where I can find a decent jewelry store around here?"

"Jewelry?"

"Engagement rings."

"Shit. You're already there?"

I lifted one shoulder and admitted, "I'm there. I don't know if she is quite yet, but I'd like to be prepared, just in case."

"Okay. Yeah. There's this one place Boss and I went when he got Jenn's ring. We can try it."

"Let's do that and then we'll find a cold beer."

"That is a plan I can get behind, brother."

"We're here. Now what?" I asked Preacher as I swung my leg over to get off my bike. "I'm not in the market for a new tattoo. I've already got an appointment next month with Phantom at Infidel's Ink."

"The tattoo artist who's working on Blue right now is the boy that Brea saved before she went to prison."

"Whoa," Hook said as he tilted his head so he could see around Preacher into the window of the tattoo shop behind him.

"I found him, or thought I did, but wanted to make sure before I said anything. That's where Blue comes in. I figured if we got a pretty woman on the table, it might be easier to get the guy to answer some questions. Blue led the conversation where I needed it to go, and he just told her that he was put into foster care when he was eight. The owner of the shop is his biological father. The state found him and gave him the boy less than two weeks after Brea killed his mom. He's the other man in there."

"Fuck. Couldn't you have told me this shit earlier? What the fuck are we doing here?"

"He's putting some kick-ass ink on Blue right now, and he's almost done. Let's wait until her tattoo is finished before we drop this little bomb on him, okay?"

"What little bomb?" I growled.

"He needs to come to Tenillo and meet Brea so she can have closure and get a good night's rest," Preacher explained. "That's my plan. Blue's on board to help convince him. If he doesn't agree to it, we can rent a car and she can drive him to Tenillo and bring him back."

"If he doesn't agree, she's going to drive him?" Hook

asked, confused.

"Well, we'll have to tie him up, and none of us can very well cart him home on the back of our bike, now, can we?"

"We're kidnapping him." I didn't ask, I just made an observance. Preacher had just passed that line in the sand Santa always talked about. He hadn't tiptoed either. He had jumped over it and was dancing on the other side. "You think we should fucking kidnap him."

"Only as a last resort. Jesus. Don't be so dramatic," Preacher huffed as he turned and walked back into the tattoo shop.

"He's got a good plan. Well, all but the kidnapping part. What do you think?" Hook asked as we stared into the shop at the guy bent over Blue's extended arm.

I could see that they were talking, and there was an older man sitting at his own station who occasionally joined the conversation along with Preacher.

"I guess we should go in and be honest with the guy. Tell him what's going on with Brea - that she dreams of him almost every night because she's been worried about him all this time. We'll see what he says."

"And if he tells us to get fucked, we'll go Preacher's route."

"No. We're not going to fucking kidnap the kid. Jesus."

"I could tranq him."

"I'm surrounded by fucking psychos. Complete nutbags."

I walked into the tattoo shop, and when the older man stood up to greet me, I introduced myself and shook his hand. Hook did the same thing as I walked closer to the table and looked at Blue's new tattoo.

I watched the artist clean the excess ink off with a paper towel before Blue lifted her arm and stared at the new piece.

"I love it," Blue told him. "You're the shit."

"Thanks," the kid told her with a grin.

"Let me pay you real quick," Blue told him as she reached into her back pocket for cash.

"I've got it," I told her as I pulled out my wallet. "How much?"

"$75 today," the guy told me. I handed him a hundred dollar bill and told him to keep the change. He thanked me and then asked, "Is there anything else I can do for y'all? I've got a couple of free hours. My next appointment cancelled."

"I'd like to ask you a question, if you don't mind." I watched Blue move around uncomfortably in her chair and realized she knew what I was about to get into with this kid. When he looked up at me curiously, I blurted out, "I'm in love with the woman that rescued you years ago, and I'm here to ask if you'll meet her so she can get some closure about what happened that night."

"What?" the man behind me barked.

"Shit. I could have done that so much better," I muttered.

"What he's saying is that my friend Brea is the woman who stopped your mother from hurting you that day when the police took you away. She never knew what happened to you after the cops came, and she's been worried about it since then," Blue told him. "I'm sorry to blindside you, but we wanted to make sure it was really you and assure that you weren't all fucked up somehow."

"She has nightmares almost every night. She dreams that she couldn't stop the woman, and she ends up killing both of you. She wakes up gasping for air like that woman is choking her all over again. We just thought . . ." I trailed off when the guy interrupted me.

"She used to do that," the guy said softly as his hand came up and touched his tattooed throat. "I remember that day and the lady you're talking about. The cops cuffed her and took her away in a car while the paramedics were putting me into an ambulance."

"She thinks about you all the time," Preacher told him. "She doesn't know where you are or if you had a good life, and I think it's eating at her."

"She saved me. I remember thinking I was going to die that day. I knew my mom was higher than I'd ever seen her, and I just knew she was going to kill me that time."

"Oh, honey," Blue said as she reached out and picked up his hand. "I'm so sorry to bring back those memories. We just want to help our friend."

"I'd like to meet her," Joseph, the boy's dad, said as he

stepped behind his son and put his hand on his shoulder and squeezed it in support. "Even if Jake doesn't want to, I'd like to meet her. She saved my son's life."

"Her name is Brea. She has a daughter that's probably just a few years older than you. Her name is MaryLea, but we all call her Sis. Brea's real funny and smart. She's got a heart bigger than Texas."

"And a mouth to match," Preacher interrupted. "I'm just saying . . ."

I let out a sigh and spoke over Preacher, "She has these French bulldogs that she treats like royalty. One of them is a total crackhead who has to be sedated, or he'll never stop running around the house at full speed. She's absolutely perfect in every way, and someday, I'm going to marry her."

"She's my best friend," Hook told the guy. "She talks shit like no other, but when it comes down to it, she's the one you want on your side. Obviously."

Hook let out an uncomfortable laugh, and I heard Blue snort as she tried to stifle hers.

"He's right about the talking shit thing. That woman makes me fucking crazy, but she's good people. I found you to help her out. So, if you can, we'd like for you to come to Tenillo and meet her someday soon. Like today. Maybe tomorrow."

"I want to meet her."

"I'll come with you, son. I bet your mom would like to come too," Joseph said softly. He looked up at me and said, "His birth mother took off with him when she found out I was seeing someone else, and I didn't know how to find her. My wife and I searched, but there was no trace of them. We even saved up and hired a PI, but he had no luck either. She'd never registered him for school or anything, and the state wasn't any fucking help. We never gave up, and when the authorities called us and said he was in the hospital, we couldn't get to him fast enough."

"We're closed tomorrow. Can we follow you back?"

"That would be great," I told him honestly. "It's going to be one hell of a surprise."

18

BREA

"Hi!" I was surprised to see Chef at the window of the coffee truck. I hadn't expected him back until this afternoon. "Meet me around back?"

Chef nodded, and I was shocked to see Blue when I opened the back door of the truck.

"Well, hello," I told her as I held the door open for her to squeeze past. "What are you doing here?"

"I am your relief for the afternoon," Blue explained. "Talk to Chef. Hey, Jenn!"

"Hi," Jenn said, just as confused as I was. "I didn't realize I'd hired a new employee."

"Just a temp. I worked in a bookstore years ago and learned how to make coffee with their machines. We'll see if I remember anything."

I left Jenn and Blue to talk and stepped out of the truck to find Chef waiting for me. He pulled me into his arms and kissed me. It felt so good to be near him again that I had to resist the urge to take our kiss from an 'I've missed you' to an 'inappropriate in public' kind of kiss.

"Why's Blue here to relieve me? I mean, yeah, I've missed you, but you've only been gone a day."

"I've got a surprise for you at home."

"Did you already go inside?" I asked as I felt my heart start to race. "I've got a surprise for you too."

"Well, just into the living room. Hook and Preacher are waiting for us. Who's in there with you and Jenn today?"

"Kitty. Bug was here for a while, but he wasn't feeling well, so he had Kitty come in and relieve him. He went to the clinic to see Frankie."

"She does STD testing?"

"His throat hurts."

"Again, I ask . . . she does STD testing?" Chef said before he laughed loudly. "Shit. And he's not even here for me to insult. Talk about a missed opportunity."

"What's my surprise?"

"Well, if I told you, it wouldn't really be a surprise. Let's go home." Chef tugged on my hand and pulled me toward the street. I saw his motorcycle parked along the curb.

"Let me get my purse at least," I told him with a laugh as I pulled away. "Hold on."

"Okay. I'll meet you at the bike."

I turned around and went back into the trailer. Jenn and Blue stopped talking abruptly and watched as I stepped over to grab my purse off the shelf.

"What? Telling secrets?"

"No," Blue told me. "We were saying shitty things about you, and you suddenly showed back up. Were your ears burning?"

"Well, continue, by all means," I told them with a laugh, knowing Blue was lying. Neither of them were the backstabbing type. "I'm going home to show my man what we worked on yesterday."

"You got him a surprise too?" Blue asked. "Isn't that funny? I bet his wins."

"I didn't realize it was a competition, but mine wins, hands down. Believe me. It's going to put a smile on his face for a long time."

"And yours." Jenn smiled. "Boss has a great chiropractor. I'll send you his information."

"I won't need it. I've seen my guy lift a full-grown man over his head. He can put me wherever I need to be, and I'm sure I'll like it just fine."

Jenn tipped her cup up and munched on a piece of that Sonic ice we loved so much before she laughed and said, "Yeah, I bet you will."

"What did I miss?"

"Frankie's got it on video, Blue. Words just can't describe what you missed."

"She better delete that, or I'm going to kick her ass."

"This I've got to see. I'll talk to you later, Brea. Call me tonight if you come up for air."

"Maybe tomorrow. I think Chef missed me."

"Okay, Pickle. Before we go in, I need to talk to you for a minute. This surprise we've got for you came from Preacher. He put the ball in motion, and I rolled with it because I think it's going to be good for you."

"Now I'm a little afraid," I admitted. "What's going on?"

I heard the front door open and saw Hook and Paula walk out onto my front porch followed by Preacher. They walked down the steps toward us and were standing close by before they said anything.

"Hey, babe," Hook said as he pulled me close to his side and hugged me against him. "Let's do dinner at our house tomorrow, okay?"

"Sure. I'll tell Sis."

"Call me later?" Paula wore the strangest smile.

"Yeah, sure. Is everything okay?"

"Everything is great, Brea. We'll talk later."

Preacher didn't say a word as he got on his bike and started it up. By the time Hook and Paula were settled, he was already headed down the street toward his house out on Pop's compound. Chef and I watched Hook and Paula pull out of my driveway and turn towards their house before I looked at him directly and asked, "What's going on, Chef?"

"Come in the house, Pickle, and you'll understand. I

love you. You know that, right?"

"You're freaking me out. I love you too."

Chef held my hand and didn't let it go as he held the door open for me to walk past him into the house. There was a man about our age sitting on a barstool with a beer in front of him. Next to him was a woman who looked just a few years younger. The two of them stayed seated, but the young man with them stood and walked toward us as Chef nudged me forward and closed the door behind us.

"Hi," I said a little uncomfortably, wondering who these strangers were that were in my house.

"You don't recognize me, do you? I'll admit, I do look a bit different since you last saw me," the young man said as he got closer. "You look just like I remember. You're still beautiful. Like an angel."

"You look familiar," I whispered, wondering where I'd seen this kid before. "Your eyes . . ."

"My name's Jake. I wouldn't be here today if you hadn't protected me."

"You're the boy." I was stunned in that moment of recognition as I studied his face. I felt Chef's hand at the small of my back, and I leaned against it as I reeled in shock. I took a deep breath as tears filled my eyes, and the man in front of me got blurry. "You're okay!"

"I'm better than okay, ma'am. I'm great. I've had a good life because you saved me." Jake put his arms up, and I fell into them, pulling him tightly to me as I cried. I could feel him shaking as I held him against me, and I heard the woman sitting at the bar crying right along with us. I sobbed when he whispered, "Thank you."

Chef's hand slowly moved up and down my back, comforting me as I held the boy I'd dreamed of for so long. I felt like a weight had been lifted off my shoulders. I finally felt peace after all these years.

"We wondered what happened to you. They wouldn't tell us anything, but I knew you hadn't been charged with killing her."

When I realized who Jake was, Kelly, Joseph's wife, had cried almost as hard as I had. She'd pulled me into her arms and thanked me right along with Joseph, and I realized the irony of the situation.

They were thanking me for killing someone. Granted, she was hurting a child at the time and fully deserved the ass kicking I put down on her, but she was dead. However, it was either her or the boy, and everyone in this room believed I'd done the right thing.

"I went back to prison on a parole violation," I explained. "I'd already missed two appointments with my PO, but the cops finding me there in a known drug house was the last nail in the coffin. Luckily, I stayed clean and turned my life around when I got out."

"I'm glad to hear it," Joseph said with a smile.

"It looks like you've got a good life too," Jake said as he motioned around the house with one hand. He was sitting at the kitchen table with the rest of us, but he was holding Sis's possum and hedgehog in his other arm. They were piled on top of each other sleeping, content with their spot against his chest.

"There was a bump or two, but I'm happy now," I said as I snuggled in a little closer under Chef's arm. "Did it take you long to get settled in with your dad?"

"It was a rough road for a few years," Kelly said as she reached over and lightly nudged Jake's shoulder. "It's understandable, but he had some trust issues where women were concerned."

"I can't imagine why," Chef said sarcastically.

"I know, right? But Mom helped me get past that. I'm engaged. Her name's Caroline. We've been together since high school. She's finishing up her last semester in Austin right now, but she's excited to meet you. I told her all about you, although I may have embellished a bit. She's going to be shocked to see that you don't have wings or a halo."

"I'm sure she'll adjust," I told Jake with a laugh. "I have them, though. I dressed as an angel for one year when Sis was a devil. I think the costumes are still in the attic somewhere. We get dressed up for trick or treaters every Halloween."

"Oh, gee. Something to look forward to," Chef mumbled. I poked him in the ribs and he grunted. "You probably dress up the dogs, too, don't you?"

"Um, yeah," I said sarcastically. "Why wouldn't I?"

"Of course you do."

"Will you come to our wedding? Your friends too. I really liked talking to Blue and Preacher. Hook seems like a funny guy, and his girlfriend is a riot."

"I'll let them know they're invited, but yeah, I'm sure we'll all be there."

"I'll get your addresses later so I can have Caroline send the invites out when it's time."

"That would be great. I'd love to come!" I told them honestly. "I love weddings as long as I don't have to plan them or take pictures of them."

"You do photography?"

"It's a hobby of mine. I've done plenty of weddings, but they're not my favorite. Too much going on and I'd rather enjoy the ceremony from the audience."

"I think it's time we got out of your hair." Joseph said from across the table. "If we leave now, we'll get home at a decent hour. Kelly's got work tomorrow morning, and she's a bear if she doesn't get her sleep."

"Some of us can't sleep until noon everyday," Kelly told him with a frown. "Can you two come to visit us soon? We'd love to have you for dinner."

"Pick a day, and we'll be there," Chef assured them. "And you're welcome here anytime, of course."

"It was great meeting you, Brea," Jake said as he put the animals down by his feet. He stood up and walked around the table, and I stood to give him another hug. "I'm glad you have a happy life. I always wondered about you.

246

Chef said that you have terrible dreams about me. Maybe that will stop now."

"I hope so."

Chef and I stood on the porch and watched the family drive off. Once their taillights were gone, I turned in his arms and put my face up for a kiss.

"Can I have my surprise now?"

"Can you take me to Preacher's first?"

"He's had enough togetherness for a while, Pickle. Let's give him until tomorrow. I'll take you over, and you can start his day off with a bang."

"I'm gonna hug him."

"Oh, he's just gonna love that."

I laughed and laid my head on Chef's chest. "Thank you, Marques. Seeing him all grown up and happy makes my heart lighter somehow."

"I hoped it would. It may not make the dreams stop completely, but maybe it will help them ease up."

"It's so good to see that they have this sweet family. They seem happy, and Jake's so well adjusted. He's in a long-term relationship, and he's found a profession he loves. He's even working with his dad every day. I can tell just by talking to them that he loves Kelly like she's his own mother."

"Yeah. They definitely seem happy." We stood there together enjoying the sunset for a few minutes, wrapped up in each other, and Chef finally asked, "Didn't you have a surprise for me too?"

"I do."

"And it's in the bedroom?"

"Yeah. That's why I wouldn't let you go in there earlier."

"Show me."

"Give me 30 minutes," I told him. "Don't come in there until I text you, okay?"

"Okay," Chef drawled slowly as I pulled away and started into the house.

"You're gonna love this. Believe me."

19

CHEF

I looked at my phone when it vibrated and was happy to see it was a text from Brea letting me know I could finally come into the bedroom. I'd heard the water come on a while ago and then turn off when she finished her shower, but there'd been nothing for at least 20 minutes.

I'd already settled the dogs in with Sis and made sure that the front and back doors were locked for the night. There wasn't much more puttering around I could do out here. I was anxious to get in there and see this surprise she had planned for me.

"Fuck, I hope she's naked," I muttered as I walked down the hall. "If she's not, she's gonna be in about 10 seconds."

I pushed the bedroom door open and was shocked when I realized she wasn't on the bed. I saw movement out of the corner of my eye. I turned to look and found a sight that instantly made my cock so hard, it was painful.

I stood there staring at the woman in front of me as I unbuttoned my pants and stepped out of my boots. I never took my eyes off of her as I finished getting undressed. I stroked my cock as I moved closer, and I realized she was watching my hand move up and down intently.

"Well, isn't this just the prettiest thing I've ever seen?" I asked as I reached out and ran my finger up the sole of Brea's bare foot. She jerked it back, and I smiled when she started swaying from just that one motion. "You bought us a new toy."

"You said you wanted one for your sex cave, so the girls and I went to that store out on the loop and picked one up."

I looked up and saw the eye bolt in the ceiling and smiled.

"Who did you have install it? I need to buy them a beer."

"I installed it. Well, me and the girls. If this works out like I hope, we're going to put one in Hook and Paula's bedroom next weekend. Jenn's not quite on board yet, but she thinks Boss might jump at the chance."

I chuckled for a second, imagining just how quickly Boss would crawl his ass up into the attic to install one. "I believe Boss would do backflips if she ever suggested it."

"I'll make sure and tell her that," Brea whispered as she watched me stroke my cock. "She tested out the seat when they were helping me hang it."

"Oh, I bet that was fun."

"They got me situated so that it should be just right for you. It was a little traumatic. I ended up hanging by one leg like a trapeze artist, but we worked it out."

"I bet that was funny."

"Frankie's got it on video. That's what was going on when you called."

"I need to see that."

"Like hell you do."

I stood there staring at Brea's naked body, my eyes drinking in her skin, stopping between her legs as I moved just a little closer.

"There's ties here for my legs, and they're adjustable for height. My arms too. Or just my hands," Brea rambled as she watched me. "I can lay all the way back or sit up. There are all sorts of options."

"All sorts, huh?"

"Yeah."

"I like the restraints for your legs . . . I want to play with those first."

"Okay," Brea agreed.

"We still going with sauerkraut?"

"Yep, but I can't imagine you'll be hearing me say it anytime soon."

"I hope not," I said as I reached out and grabbed her knee. I pulled on it and she spun around until I caught her knee again when she'd made a full circle. "I like this."

"A good surprise?"

"I can't think of a single way you could top it," I admitted. "Not a single way."

I reached up and adjusted the leg restraints a little lower before I wrapped one around Brea's thigh. Once I had her legs secured and she was spread wide in front of me, I gave her a slight push, and she spun again. I stopped the motion once her back was to me and nibbled on her neck while I restrained her hands.

"Comfortable?" I murmured when I was done.

"Yeah," Brea panted softly. "Excited."

"Oh, so am I, Pickle. So am I."

"How's she doing?" Preacher asked as we got settled in on the back porch.

I picked up Danee and Ripley and set them on the couch beside me before I settled the freaking possum *and* the hedgehog down next to them.

"Well, she's been sleeping soundly for about 10 hours now, so my guess is she's doing alright," I told him honestly. Brea had a quiet night and hadn't woken me up once. When I got out of bed this morning, I'd even leaned over and rested my hand on her back just to make sure she was breathing. She was sleeping so hard that I wasn't sure she'd even rolled over in the night.

"How did she take the news about you and Hook?"

I slowly turned and glared at Preacher. He pulled his lips between his teeth as he resisted a smile but couldn't hold it. He laughed so hard and for so long, I wondered how many times I'd have to hit him to get him quiet.

"I can't believe he told you about that."

"He didn't tell me, Sis did. It was a group text. I guess she forgot to include you."

"She must have."

"How did you know Brea was the one for you? I mean, you obviously loved your wife, so how did you replace her with Brea?"

"I didn't replace her," I scoffed. "That's impossible. She has a place in my heart and always will. So does my daughter. But now, so does Brea. And Sis, too, of course. Even these goddamn dogs and rodents have one."

"You've never had a woman double-cross you?"

"I married young, but I had other girls before my wife and a few when I got out of prison. Two of them fucked me over, but not too bad. One cheated, and the other lied. You get that with all kinds of people, though - friends, lovers, whatever. Why?"

"I was raised to believe that a man should love one woman for all of his life. End of story. You commit yourself to that one person, and that's it. You better choose carefully or you're fucked."

"And why exactly are you telling me this? Are you saying you don't *approve* of me and Brea? Because if that's the . . ."

"I could give a lesser shit where you dip your wick, Chef. Jesus. I'm just trying to wrap my head around there being more than one person out there for each of us."

"There's a million, if you're looking. You can adapt to

anything. When you're committed and happy, or even if you're not, you don't look for other potential mates. After the one you love has been gone for some time, it's natural to look for another partner. People aren't meant to be alone. If your religion told you that, then it's fucked."

"We committed a sin, and we paid the price for it," Preacher said in a voice barely above a whisper. "I paid and so did she, but she got past it. I didn't think we were supposed to do that."

"Is that why you don't like women? Don't get me wrong, man. If there's another reason, I'm open to that too. You're my friend, and, like you said, I could give a lesser shit where you dip your wick."

"You think I like men?"

"I didn't say that, but if you do, more power to ya."

"I never did that in prison, you know."

"I am not here to talk about that shit," I said emphatically.

"That's what kept me in prison. I went down for two years for car theft." Preacher sighed. "Defended myself a little too forcefully and killed a man. Two, actually. For the same thing, just at different times."

"Okay," I said softly as I looked out over the yard. "Why are we talking about this?"

"I thought I'd love Carrie until the day I died, but I barely remember her now."

"Carrie's the one you were seeing when you got

busted, right?'

"Yeah. Her daddy had a hissy fit and said that I stole his car."

"She let him?"

"You respect your elders, even when they're assholes."

"Bullshit."

"I always thought that was why she married the man her dad had picked out for her. She married him six months after I got convicted. Almost six months to the day. Big wedding. Her dad sent me pictures, a whole stack of 'em."

"What a fucking asshole."

"I looked into her as soon as I got out. I thought I'd find her, sweep her away, and we'd live happily ever after."

"Did you find her?"

"Yeah, I found her," Preacher said bitterly. "I was fucking stupid. I'd been gone for 26 years. I was as good as dead to her."

"Did you talk to her?"

"Yeah, I did. About two months after I got out. I took the bike Pop and I built and left town. Didn't tell anyone where I was going. I watched her house for a few days, got their schedules down, and waited for her old man to leave before I knocked on the door." Preacher leaned forward and rested his elbows on his knees as he stared unseeingly out over the yard. "She recognized me right off. Looked afraid at first, but then she invited me in for coffee like we'd just talked the day before or something. I went inside and her grandson was in a high chair waiting for breakfast."

"Ouch."

"I asked her how she'd been, and she said she had four kids and two grandkids. They'd gone to Hawaii for their 25th wedding anniversary the year before, and she showed me a picture of the beach I'd always said she and I would visit some day."

"What a bitch."

"Nah. She said she thought of me while she was there and wondered if I'd ever get to see it."

"I asked her to go with me so I could see it myself, and she looked at me like I'd lost my fucking mind. She loved her husband and her family, and I get that. But how could she just go right along living the life we were supposed to have together?"

"Okay, aside from the fact that she married that fucker right after you left, what kind of selfish son of a bitch are you to think that a teenage girl should stop living her life while you're locked up for a quarter of a century?"

"I was only supposed to be gone for two years."

"Oh, yeah. That does change things, doesn't it?"

"I thought maybe she was a hostage or something."

"Is that when all this conspiracy shit you buy into started? When you thought he railroaded you so she could marry that guy? You concluded she was only staying with him because she had to while she waited on you?"

"He *did* railroad me. The man she married was the son of a man he wanted to do business with. Up until two years ago, they had a very successful partnership."

"What happened two years ago?"

"The government randomly decided they needed to be audited since they were a publicly traded company. Turns out, her daddy was misusing funds, lying to the board members, buying hookers with what was supposed to be charitable donations, and kicking puppies in his spare time. He was the preacher in the church I went to growing up, and let me just say, they were appalled. The whole congregation was stunned when his misdeeds came to light. He swore it was a set-up, but no one believed him. He's serving time for embezzlement now."

"He said it was a set-up?"

"Karma dry fucked him in the ass with a cactus, I guess."

"Is your middle name Karma?"

"Well, it was a few years ago," Preacher admitted with a grin.

"How'd this conversation go from a discussion on one's soulmates in a lifetime to someone getting fucked with a cactus?"

"I think I walked out at just the wrong time," I heard Brea say from behind us. I turned and looked back at the door just in time to see Brea do an about-face to go back inside.

"Come here, Pickle," I chuckled. "We're not telling state secrets or anything."

"Yeah, but I have a thing for cacti and not that way."

"We weren't gonna do anything with your cactus plants, Mouth. Jeez."

"Good morning, Preacher," Brea said in that teasing tone she often used with him. "You came to start your day off by seeing me, huh? Give me some sugar, sweet stuff."

"Fuck you," Preacher grumbled.

"Talk to Brea, Preach," I suggested. "Get her take on what we were discussing. She didn't come in for that part, so she'll be impartial."

"She'll be a pain in my ass."

"Probably not as much of a pain as that cactus over there would be, but if you sass me too much before I finish my first cup of coffee, we'll find out," Brea said as she pointed out a plant that was almost as big around as my leg. "Let me put it to you like this, Preach. I love you. Simple as that. You make me fucking crazy, and most of the time, I want to punch you, but you've got a solid place in my heart. Now, is there someone I need to maim? Kill? What's going on here? What did I miss?"

"Can you find true love more than once?" I asked Brea.

"Well, yeah. Our first true loves are in those pictures on the living room mantle."

"See? A shorter version of what I said, Preach."

"Is there someone you're interested in?"

"No," Preacher snapped. "You two are just playing out some storybook love story shit, Paula and Hook seem to have made it their mission to fuck in every single building in this town, and Jenn and Boss are a combination of the two. I was wondering if I might be missing out on something. It's probably too late for me anyway."

"It's never too late," Brea encouraged him. "Don't give up."

"Don't you go yammering to your crazy coven about this shit, either, Mouth. I don't want them setting me up on dates and shit," Preacher warned.

"Oh, buddy, I'm sure none of us know a single woman worthy of you." I knew there was a double entendre there, and I was sure Preacher did too. "If I come across a woman that I think might interest you, I'll run it past you before I say anything to her, okay?"

"See? You're already fucking planning shit," Preacher grumbled as he stood up. The animals sitting next to me on the couch perked up and stared at him. He started for the screen door to go out into the yard rather than the door to go inside, and they all jumped off the couch and followed him. "I'm gonna go talk to Sis and her foul-mouthed bird. He's got more brains in a single feather than I'm finding on this porch."

"Have a good day, you cranky bastard!" Brea called out as we watched Preacher stomp across the yard to Sis's little house. Preacher put his hand up and flipped us off without looking back, and Brea and I both laughed. "I can't imagine what kind of woman could put up with that man's shit."

"How'd you sleep, sweetheart?"

"Like the dead. Seriously. I didn't wake up once."

"Good. Maybe yesterday helped."

"Or maybe you fucked me into a coma with that swing."

"I like that swing, Pickle," I told her with a grin. "I like it a whole lot. Before Preacher got here, I was thinking of all sorts of things to do with you in it."

"I just got out of the shower, and I wouldn't mind another spin in it." My dick got hard enough to pound nails the second she made the suggestion, and I knew she could feel it under her leg where she was seated on my lap. "I take that as a yes?"

"That's a hell yes, sweetheart. I'll follow you wherever you're going."

20

TWO WEEKS LATER

CHEF

Boss slapped his hand on the table for a call to order, and everyone sitting around it went quiet. "Okay, so a lot of shit has gone down in the last few months. I got you guys together so we could all get on the same page. Now, all of you know what happened with Sis, and we got some good information on that front before Chef fed that one guy dinner and relaxed with that last one."

There was some laughter as Boss downplayed what I'd done that night.

"I'm never eating at his house. That's for damn sure," Captain told us through his laughter.

"Brea's a fine cook. We'll just have to make sure Chef stays out of the kitchen," Boss said as the chatter died down. "We have been successful at gathering quite a bit of intel by using Jenn's truck. Hook and Chef have been eavesdropping at the gym, and we've gotten quite a bit of information from the bugs that Frankie and Brea planted at the car dealership as well as with Jon Bentley, but not enough to answer all of our questions yet."

"The biggest question is why are the two of them even talking? They've got nothing in common. They're not even close in age. Fairchild isn't in the market for real estate, and Jon Bentley is clearly in love with that foreign sports car he drives around, so he's not likely to buy a new car anytime soon," Santa told the table. "I had a look around both places, and their security is garbage. Me or Kitty could get in and out with no one the wiser about as easy as breathing. The man doesn't have a security system anywhere except his accounting area, and even that's laughable. He's got cameras from that doorbell outfit, not even decent shit."

"Is there a reason you'd need to break in?" Captain asked.

"Well, not right now, but it helps to be prepared."

"Chef and Hook got a tip at the gym about Fairchild searching for a car, but we don't know if that's because he wants to recoup his money or what. It just seemed weird that he was willing to threaten a cop rather than go down to the precinct and ask about the location of one of his leased vehicles," Hook told our group. "Made no sense to me. If he lost one, insurance would take care of that shit."

"I've got Wrecker watching the cop that Hannigan mentioned. Harrison is his last name. Seems legit, so we don't know what she has on him other than she helped the principal decide to keep the cops out of a bullying case he was involved in at the high school," Boss explained. "There's been two more girls that have gone missing since they attempted to abduct Sis."

"She wasn't the only one that got taken that night, right?" Bug asked. "I thought I heard you say something about another team."

"There's at least one, but maybe two more teams of men picking up women. We got the one that night, but while we were busy, two more girls went missing. Now, the information we got on the last time each girl was seen makes it a possibility that it's just one other team of guys doing it. It would be cutting it close, considering the locations in town, but it could be done."

"Boss had me and Pitbull run a scenario like we were the ones doing the kidnapping. Made me fucking sick to my stomach," Kitty complained. "Just the thought of some scumbag carting women around like they're cattle is enough to make me see red. Fucking assholes."

"Speaking of Pitbull, Blue's working at his bar. He's got great security, but if a few of you guys could go show her your support now and then, I know she'd appreciate it," Boss said as he looked around the table at the single men. "She's well protected there, but it might be nice for her to see some friendly faces, you know?"

"Wait. So, she decided to stay in town?" Preacher asked.

"She's staying. It was a spur-of-the-moment decision, and she's not saying why - just that she felt like it. Knowing my sister, I wouldn't put it past her for her spontaneous streak to be the one and only reason, but I feel like there's something more going on that she isn't telling me. Will you keep an ear out, and see if your old ladies mention anything?" Santa asked us. "I'm not worried yet, but I probably should be, if that makes any sense."

"How are things going with the Infidels? I talked to Jackie the other day at her shop, and she said there was some movement out there," Captain told us.

"Are you dating her?" I asked, remembering that I'd seen him there when I went to arrange for Brea's gifts. Captain didn't say anything, he just shrugged. "She's a beautiful woman. I was just being nosy."

"Too much time with Mouth. She's wearing off on you. And those other women are too. Walking around with your heads in the clouds in some sex haze," Preacher complained.

"We need to find someone to put you in a sex haze," Bug suggested. "Might just chill you out, brother."

"There's shit going on all around us. I need to be vigilant, not chilled out. Apparently, I'm gonna have to be the ringmaster since Boss is always smiling and shit now," Preacher told us.

I looked over at Boss, and sure enough, he was smiling. "Honestly, I guess that's all I've got for discussion. You all know Pop's doing fine. He's as cantankerous as ever."

"He's more so now than before, I swear. Grumpy old bastard," Kitty complained. "Got on my ass about my music choices the other day. Who the fuck doesn't love Kid Rock?"

"Paula loves Kid Rock. I don't mind him," Hook said conversationally. "I like Eminem better, though."

I shook my head at the two and argued, "Dr. Dre. You fools have no fucking taste."

"Well, now that we've started to delve into the finer points of our favorite rappers, I think it's safe to say our meeting has concluded. I'm going to head home and find Jenn and a plate of food."

Hook and I stood at the same time, both of us clearly eager to see Brea and Paula.

"I guess we'll meet again in a few weeks, if not sooner," Boss announced. "Better not be before. I'm sick of weird shit happening. We need some peace for a while."

"And that's how you jinx us," Captain complained. "Fuck, man. You know better than to say those kinds of things when it's quiet."

I listened to my brothers complain as we closed up the well house and walked to Boss and Jenn's. Tonya, Hook's big cat, must have heard us from her outdoor pen because she roared a few times as if she wanted to join the conversation.

Once we were inside, I found Brea sitting at the bar with Blue and the other girls. There was food spread all along the counters, and my brothers started filling their plates and making conversation.

"Hey, Pickle. Did you have a good chat with the girls?"

"I did, but we're having a crazy discussion. Maybe you and Hook could referee with all of your scientific knowledge. You, too, Boss," Brea said loud enough for him to hear her where he was standing with Jenn. "Blue said something that sounds good in theory, but we aren't sure if it would actually work."

"What's the question, Blue?" Boss asked. I noticed that the rest of the men were listening and knew they'd be putting in their two cents right along with us.

"Okay, hypothetically, if you wanted to bury a body,

you should bury them in a deep hole standing on their feet. That way, the ground-penetrating radar wouldn't detect a body. It would only pick up the top of the skull, and they could just explain that away, right?"

"Well, yeah, they probably wouldn't think much of it. It could be a rock or whatever. But cadaver dogs would find it," Captain told her.

"Okay, but here's the rest. Bury the body upright, and pack it with dirt. Make sure there's quite a bit on top and then bury an animal. A dog or whatever, just like someone buried a family pet when it died," Blue explained, using her hands to talk as she always did, gesticulating wildly like she was arranging a burial plot right there at the table. "The cadaver dogs would only smell the dead animal, and if the cops *did* dig, they'd find the carcass and assume that was it. They'd fill the hole back up before they ever dug deep enough to find the corpse."

I looked around and every single man in the room was still and silent, listening to Blue. We all stood with our mouths hanging open in shock at her idea, wondering why in the hell we hadn't thought of that before.

"Don't you have a pet cemetery out there on your property?" I quietly asked Hook. He slowly nodded, and we both looked at Boss.

"Holy shit," Boss muttered. "Where did you come up with that, Blue?"

"TikTok."

"They talk about how to bury bodies on TikTok?" Boss asked.

"I thought it was just people dancing and shit on there," Santa said as he picked up his phone.

Hook chimed in, "Paula's always watching these shirtless guy videos and sending them to all the other girls. Jenn sends cute animals and shit, but I've never seen anything else worthwhile."

Blue shrugged as she slid off the barstool to go and make her plate. "I don't know. I just thought it was interesting. Would it work?"

"I'm sure we'll have a reason to find out sooner or later," Boss remarked as he walked across the kitchen with Jenn to get plates of their own.

"You gonna bury me upright and put a dog on my head, Pickle?"

"Maybe Preacher but not you. I love you."

"I love you too. And I'll keep in mind just how crazy you women are before I ever piss you off enough for you to consider how you'll bury me."

"All those muscles, and brains to go with 'em. That's my Chef."

"Have any of you guys looked at the DNA results thing Jenn hooked us up with?" Captain asked. He put his hand up and shook his head before he growled, "Preacher, don't start. I'm not listening to that shit tonight."

"Hmph," Preacher snorted but turned his attention

back to the plate in front of him without saying anything else.

"I haven't looked at it again. I don't have any family left," Bug remarked casually as if it didn't bother him at all. "I guess maybe there's cousins out there or something, but that's probably it."

"I got an anonymous message asking me all sorts of shit. I can't figure out who it's coming from, though. I think they've blocked me from seeing their identity for some reason."

"I can look into it for you, maybe figure out something," Preacher suggested.

"What did the message say exactly?" Boss asked.

"Just asking me where I went to school, what I did after I graduated . . . shit like that."

"Maybe an ex-girlfriend?" Jenn suggested.

"Probably not. We gave them fake names, remember?" Paula reminded her. "Just initials and a fresh email address."

"I didn't answer. I probably won't either," Captain said with a shrug. "I changed it to show my name though. That's probably how they found me.

"I should look at mine, and see if there's anyone there," Kitty told us. "Maybe I've got some family somewhere who don't know I used to be a thief and that they're supposed to hate me."

"I'll look into it for you," Paula told Kitty. "I'll see if I can find anyone. Anybody else want me to check theirs? I've got all the passwords saved on my laptop."

"Look at mine, will you? I don't know what all the leaves and shit are for, but it says I've got more than 30," Captain told her.

"Maybe someone died and left you money, and there's a long-lost relative trying to help reach you," Preacher suggested.

"Shit. Like anyone's gonna chase someone down to *give* them money," Santa argued. "It's more likely someone wanting money. Blue and I looked through ours and laughed at the family we found on there. Thank God it's anonymous."

"Isn't that the truth?" Blue grumbled from across the table. "Cousins crawling out of the woodwork."

"I told my mom we were part French, and Dad said that she's trying to make French food now. He's pretty pissed at me," I told my friends. "All he wants is home cooking, and she's making weird sauces and shit."

"We can overnight him some of Jenn's desserts," Brea suggested.

"Why don't we take some to them instead?"

"We? You want me to go?"

"I do. I want you to meet my parents," I told her as I leaned over and gave her a kiss. "I've told them all about you, and they're dying to meet you."

"Oh shit," Brea whispered. "I'm too old to meet parents. Do you know how stressful that is?"

"How stressful?" Preacher asked. "Stressful enough to get you to stop yammering so I can digest my food?"

"Hook, did you have any dogs cross over the rainbow bridge today?" Brea called down the table. "I need one for a hole I'm about to fill."

"I'd like to see you dig a hole deep enough for me," Preacher dared.

"Chef would help if I asked him to," Brea taunted him.

Preacher seemed offended and had to argue. "Like hell, he would!"

"I might have to let you do that all by yourself, Pickle," I told her. Brea leaned over and whispered in my ear, and I got a visual about exactly which position she was describing on that swing, and my cock got hard. "Well, some new information has come to light, and I think I may need to go buy a new shovel before I get started."

"Walking around with a smile on your face and your head in the clouds!" Preacher said loudly. "All fucking three of ya!"

"I told you we'd find someone to give you that smile," Bug warned Preacher.

"I'm going to eat out on the porch with the fucking herd of animals," Preacher grumbled as he picked up his plate. "No one better come out there unless they want some peace and quiet!"

We all snickered and giggled as we watched Preacher go. I was shocked when Blue pushed her chair out and picked up her plate. "Y'all are just going to let him go off alone while we're all in here laughing and cutting up? Did any of you ever think that maybe he *wants* someone to ask him to fucking stay? Assholes."

There was silence as we watched Blue storm out of the kitchen and join Preacher on the back porch where Jenn had all the animals penned up. I glanced around the table and saw Jenn and Paula smiling, and when I looked at Brea, she was smiling too.

"What was that about?" I asked in Brea's ear as I pulled her close to my side.

"Another one bites the dust," Brea whispered back with a grin. "Oh, how the mighty will fall."

"Was I mighty? I know I fell," I whispered before I gave her a kiss. "Love you, Pickle."

"Love you, too, Marques."

COMING SOON

Tavin (Conner Brothers Construction, Book 5) - COMING SEPTEMBER 15TH, 2021!

Tavin and London have been together for a while now, but life and responsibilities are tearing them apart.

With London traveling all over the world for her career, and Tavin stuck in Rojo, Texas for his, the two of them have to make do with precious few stolen moments leaving both of them wanting more.

London starts to doubt the life choices she's made and knows she can't be happy so far away from home. Is it too late for her and Tavin to salvage their relationship?

Tavin can't leave his family to follow the woman he loves, and life at home without her has started to wear on his patience and make him question the plans he had laid out for his future.

Follow Tavin and London as they find their way back to each other and weather the stress, uncertainty, and danger that comes with the choices they make in the fifth book of the Conner Brothers Construction series.

**This book is shorter than the other stories in this series. Although it is the full story of Tavin and London that readers have been waiting for, and their story needed to be told, it's not quite as long as the other books that are available.

For that reason, I've released it at a lower price point in both the digital and printed version. I hope you enjoy their story and another trip to Rojo to catch up on the family we've all grown to love.**

Please take just a few minutes to leave a review of this book on Amazon and feel free to share the link with your friends. I enjoy discussing my books and characters and would love to hear from you.

Check out Cee Bowerman on Facebook. You can also find information about the author and her books on www.ceebowermanbooks.com.

About the Author

Cee Bowerman is proud, lifelong resident of Texas. She is married to her own long-haired, tattooed biker and is the proud mom to three mostly adult kids - a daughter and two sons. She believes in love, second chances, rescue dogs, and happily ever after.

Cee received her first romance novel along with a bag of other books from her granny when she was recovering from surgery at 15. She has been hooked on reading romances ever since. For years, she had a dream of writing her own series of stories, but motherhood and all the other grown up responsibilities kept getting in the way. Luckily, with the support of her family and the encouragement of her son, she purchased a computer and let her dreams become a reality.

Printed in Great Britain
by Amazon